CALL ACROSS THE SEA

KATHY KACER

annick press
toronto + berkeley

We acknowledge the support of the Canada Council for the Arts and the
Ontario Arts Council, and the participation of the Government of Canada/la
participation du gouvernement du Canada for our publishing activities.

Library and Archives Canada Cataloguing in Publication

Title: Call across the sea / Kathy Kacer.
Names: Kacer, Kathy, 1954- author.
Series: Kacer, Kathy, 1954- Heroes quartet.
Description: Series statement: Heroes quartet
Identifiers: Canadiana (print) 20200331248 | Canadiana (ebook)
20200331256 | ISBN 9781773214788
   (hardcover) | ISBN 9781773214795 (softcover) | ISBN 9781773214801
(HTML) | ISBN 9781773214818
   (Kindle) | ISBN 9781773214825 (PDF)
Classification: LCC PS8571.A33 C34 2021 | DDC jC813/.54—dc23

Published in the U.S.A. by Annick Press (U.S.) Ltd.
Distributed in Canada by University of Toronto Press.
Distributed in the U.S.A. by Publishers Group West.

Printed in Canada

annickpress.com
kathykacer.com

Also available as an e-book. Please visit annickpress.com/ebooks for more details.

MIX
Paper from
responsible sources
FSC
www.fsc.org   FSC® C103567

For Gabi, Jer, Jake, and Ness—
may they always be brave.

—K.K.

The future depends on what you do today.

—Mahatma Ghandi

CHAPTER 1

Salty sea air filled Henny's lungs. She tightened her grip on the steering wheel and made a sharp turn downwind, taking the boat in a wide circle to avoid the waves swelling in white-capped peaks. A strong wind rushed by her face, blowing her blond curls nearly straight back. The warm summer sun beat down from a cloudless blue sky.

"How does it look out there, Far?" she called out to her father, who stood at the bow of the boat, clutching one of the masts and gazing out at the water. He turned, raised his thumb in approval, and pointed her onward toward their destination, the Drogden Lighthouse sitting at the south end of the channel in open water. Far was a naval officer in Copenhagen,

Denmark. As head of the Danish Lighthouse and Buoy Service, his job was to bring supplies out to the lighthouse on a weekly basis—sometimes twice a week, depending on need. Henny, now sixteen, had been accompanying her father on these supply runs for years.

Far had taught her to sail almost before she could walk. The channel they sailed, between Denmark and Sweden, was Henny's playground. When others wanted to go shopping or to cafés, or even to school dances, Henny wanted to be on the water. She was as comfortable and capable at the wheel as she was riding a bicycle. This boat, the *Gerda III*, was Henny's home away from home. She knew every inch of its forty feet and twenty tons: the double-mast sail, the hold below the deck where supplies were stored, each wooden beam and gunnel, each brass knob. *Gerda III* was like a sister to her—more human than many people she knew. With a gentle nudge upwind or downwind, she could coax Gerda in any direction. She could ride her out to the sea, fast and far. But she wasn't always the one in full control. When the channel was very rough, Gerda was the one in charge, taking Henny up and up to the crest of a wave, and then dropping her down the other side, her heart diving into her stomach. *Like riding a wild horse,*

Henny thought. At those times, all she could do was hang on and trust that the boat knew what she was doing and would keep her safe. So far, Gerda had not let her down.

Otto entered the small cabin at the helm of the boat where Henny was standing behind the wheel, Gerhardt right behind him. The two crewmembers, both hired by the navy as engineers, had been sailing aboard Gerda for almost as long as her father had held his position, and at least as long as Henny had been taken along on these runs. They had watched Henny grow up on the boat.

"A little rough out there," Otto said, pushing his cap back off his forehead and scratching at his chin. "For a moment, I thought I was going into the sea." He mimicked rocking back and forth on his feet, raising one leg and falling backward while his arms spiraled in wide circles.

"It would have been man overboard for sure, if I hadn't been there to save him," Gerhardt added, reaching out to steady Otto. Gerhardt was at least a foot shorter than Otto. It was comical to watch him try and catch his taller crewmate. "You're losing your touch, Henny," Gerhardt added as Otto fell on top of him and both men nearly crumpled to the floor.

Henny laughed and quickly swerved the boat

upwind in response, surprising the two and jolting them forward. Otto banged into the wall of the cabin. Far, from his position at the bow, turned and frowned at Henny. She quickly straightened out her course and waved to him. He returned to watching the water.

"I know what I'm doing, and don't you forget it," Henny said.

"Doesn't look that way to me," Otto replied, rubbing his arm. "I think we're going to have to teach her to sail all over again, don't you agree, Gerhardt?"

"All over again!" Gerhardt echoed.

Henny ignored them. The two men teased her all the time, but she really didn't mind. If Gerda was like a sister to Henny, then Otto and Gerhardt were like big brothers—annoying at times but as close as family. Henny was an only child, so it was fun to pretend that this was what it would be like to have siblings. Even Far referred to them as "the boys," though they were both at least ten years older than Henny. But they had been working side by side on Gerda for so long that they were like one person— cleaning the deck, polishing the brass, raising the sails, repairing ropes, and doing whatever else was needed. Henny had learned as much about sailing Gerda from these two as she had learned from Far, though she would never admit that to him!

Far suddenly appeared in the cabin by Henny's side. She gazed at him—tall and distinguished looking. He cut an impressive figure in his blue naval uniform with its shiny gold buttons and his dark hair tinged with gray tucked under his sailor's cap. His eyes were turquoise and attracted the light like two magnets. Henny had inherited the same deep blue-green eyes. She loved that she shared that feature with her father. Staring into his eyes was like looking at a calm sea. But not in this moment. Far's eyes looked troubled, and his brow crinkled.

"Sorry about that, Far," Henny muttered. "We were just fooling around." The crewmembers stood behind her like two guilty schoolboys, heads lowered, hands behind their backs.

Far didn't respond. He continued staring out at the horizon, his eyes fixed on some spot in the distance.

"What is it, Far?" He was never distracted or unhappy out on the water. The sea was his peaceful place. Other things might agitate him, like balancing the accounts for the lighthouse, but never out here. "What's wrong?"

Far still didn't respond, so Henny followed his gaze out onto the water, and that was when she saw it. Up ahead was a small boat, and at its helm, the flag of the Nazi Party—a black swastika against a blood-red background. The flag appeared and disappeared as the waves rose and fell, as if it were playing a game of hide-and-seek.

The swastika was not an unfamiliar sight to Henny, or to any Dane, for that matter. The Nazis had been in Denmark since 1940, when their army, under its leader Adolf Hitler, had marched into Henny's homeland and occupied it. The Danish government led by King Christian X had surrendered immediately, knowing that any kind of resistance against the powerful Nazi army was pointless. In return, Nazi Germany had "rewarded" Denmark for being so cooperative by allowing the country to keep its government in place. King Christian was still in charge. Far said that as long as the king was still in command, everything would be fine. And the king still rode his horse through the city streets on an almost daily basis, waving to his subjects as if to reassure them that all was well. So, even though Nazi troops had roamed the streets of Copenhagen for the last few years, and their flag could be seen flying from many buildings, Henny had mostly ignored them, and they ignored her and the rest of Denmark's citizens.

But now, three years into the occupation, Henny

could tell that things were changing for the worse. Here in Copenhagen, more Nazi troops could be seen marching through the streets, clomping their boots onto the pavement, and carrying their rifles out in front of them. Henny didn't really know what their increased presence meant. Nothing had happened to her personally, and she hoped it would stay that way! She just knew that, whenever those troops showed up in the streets, everyone tried to avoid them, retreating to the sidewalks or hurrying into shops. Most Danes had come to hate the Nazis and everything they stood for. Far was no exception, and Henny had learned to hate them as well. And she knew enough about what they were doing in other countries—ransacking homes, killing innocent people, overrunning governments—to be afraid of what they might do here.

So now, to see a Nazi boat out on the channel—*her* channel—scared her. The boat up ahead continued to bob up and down as if beckoning to her. A strange feeling crept through Henny, like a shiver in the dark. It was as if her personal home had suddenly been invaded. Is that what was making her father so uneasy?

"What are the Nazis doing out here?" Henny asked.

"I have no idea," Far replied. "It's bad enough they're in the city." He spat the words out as if they left a bad taste in his mouth.

"I think we should stay back from that boat," Otto said.

Henny frowned. "Why? What will they do?"

"You never know. A friend of mine had his apartment searched by a group of soldiers who practically broke down the door to get in. He was lucky he wasn't arrested. They said he was part of a group that was protesting against them."

"Was he?" Henny asked. "Protesting, I mean."

"He went to a rally, with hundreds of other people. He just stood there, watching."

"We haven't done anything," Henny said.

"Neither did my friend," replied Otto.

"I think it's best to stay out of their way," Gerhardt added.

"Agreed!" said Far. "Henny, cut the motor."

Henny slowed Gerda and let the Nazi boat take a further lead in front of them.

Far seemed to relax as the distance between the two boats increased. His shoulders dropped from up around his ears where he had been holding them, and he exhaled.

"Good riddance to them," Otto muttered.

With that, they all turned their attention back to their destination. The lighthouse was just up ahead, its tall tower, white with unmistakable red stripes, visible at a distance of forty nautical miles. For years, this lighthouse had been a traffic-control center for boats entering and leaving the Baltic Sea. It had helped steer sailors through this busy channel in all kinds of weather, night and day.

"Steer downwind," Far called out. "That's it. Now straight ahead."

Otto and Gerhardt rushed out of the cabin to ready Gerda for her arrival. Otto stood at the bow, a thick rope in his hand, while Gerhardt took his position at the stern. Henny steered the boat through the shallow, rocky entrance to the lighthouse pier, biting her lower lip and keeping her gaze on the water, searching for the perfect path to take the boat through. She finally eased Gerda up to the dock, waiting for just the right moment to cut the motor completely. Otto and Gerhardt jumped off together and quickly secured Gerda, turning the thick ropes around the base of the big metal cleats and bringing the lines up over the top, then repeating this a second time and then a third. They finished securing the boat at the exact same second, standing and grinning at one another, hands up in the air as if they had just crossed the finish line of a race in a dead heat.

Otto smiled up at Henny, who had moved out of the cabin. "You nearly missed the dock."

"I thought we were going to have to swim in," Gerhardt added.

"I'd like to see one of you two do a better job," Henny replied. "Especially in these choppy waves."

Far interrupted their banter. "Boys, help me get the supplies off the boat and up to the lighthouse." Otto and Gerhardt quickly jumped back on board. Gerhardt pulled open the door to the hold and descended the small staircase into the storage area at the bottom of the boat, emerging a moment later carrying a box. Henny followed him back down. This storage space, measuring about six feet by ten feet and only four feet high, was lined with wooden planks and dampened by the seawater that sometimes leaked in. It smelled down here, often of gasoline and sometimes of crates of fish that they carried to the lighthouse. Henny wrinkled her nose, then bent over to avoid hitting her head and reached for a box as well.

"Anything special for the lighthouse this week?" Henny asked Far, as Otto, the last one to go into the hold, emerged with a box.

"Just the usual canned goods, along with some blankets and maintenance supplies. Plus, we're bringing some newspapers. They're a few days old, but the men out here love to get caught up on the news. Henny, why don't you stay with Gerda. The boys and I will take the supplies up."

"Are you sure you don't need me?" Usually Henny carried boxes along with Otto and Gerhardt. She never minded helping.

"We can manage on our own today."

Henny handed her box over to Gerhardt and watched as he, Far, and Otto made their way up the narrow path from the pier to the lighthouse. Once they had disappeared around a bend, she sat down on the dock next to Gerda and lay on her back, staring up at the sky, shielding her eyes from the sun's glare. She had a fleeting thought about the Nazi boat, wondering if they would see it again on their trip back to the mainland. But she quickly put that thought out of her mind. This day was too beautiful to ruin with those kinds of worries. Up above, seagulls held aloft by the wind dipped and dove in coordinated circles, as if they had rehearsed this dance.

Henny was just starting to drift off to sleep when she heard footsteps dropping onto the pier, gently rocking the platform underneath her. She opened her eyes and sat up to see Far and the others approaching. Far had that same worried look on his face that he had had out on the channel—the same furrowed brow, the same troubled eyes, and the same shoulders that were beginning to creep up to his ears.

"What's wrong?" Henny jumped to her feet, looking first at her father and then at Otto and Gerhardt. The two crewmembers shook their heads simultaneously and shrugged their shoulders.

"Just some business with the staff here," Far replied. "Nothing important."

Henny didn't believe him. She wondered if it had anything to do with the Nazi boats. But before she could ask, Far changed the topic.

"Should I even ask you if you want to skipper the boat back? Perhaps one of the boys should take the wheel."

Henny jumped on board and reentered the cabin. "Gerda and I have got this," she called out.

Otto and Gerhardt ran to untie the boat from the pier, jumping back onto the boat as the motor sprung to life.

"Hold on for dear life," Otto shouted as Henny eased the *Gerda III* out into the water and headed back home.

CHAPTER 2

When Henny and her father walked through the green painted door of their modest, two-storey home, the delicious smell of meatballs with mushrooms and fried onions—one of Henny's favorite dishes—filled every corner of the house.

"Perfect timing," Mor said as she brought another platter to the table. It looked as if she was getting ready to feed an army, not just Henny and Far. "Sit down before it all gets cold." She glanced up at Far and frowned. "What's wrong?"

After docking and mooring the *Gerda III* in her berth, Far had been quieter than usual during their twenty-minute walk home. Usually, the two of them chatted about what Henny was doing in school or when they would need to go on another run to the lighthouse. That walk around the bay overlooking the channel was as familiar to Henny as being on the water with Gerda—each shop they passed, each café, each park bench. Henny had done this walk hundreds, no, probably thousands, of times. She could have done it blindfolded and still known which landmark she was passing with each step.

They had not seen any Nazi boats on their journey back to the city, so Henny wasn't sure why her father was so quiet. Was he still thinking about the Nazi boats? Whatever the reason, it made Henny feel uneasy. And now, Mor, too, could tell that something was wrong.

"It seems that the Nazis have been running boats in the channel," Far replied. He seemed reluctant to talk, as if he was still trying to figure it all out in his mind. "The staff at the lighthouse told me," he added.

So that was what he had been so upset about when he had returned to Gerda after dropping off supplies, Henny realized, glancing quickly at her father, and then turning to Mor.

"We saw a boat too. It's the first time I've seen a Nazi flag out on the water."

Mor's eyes widened and her hands rose quickly to her face. Mor was never one to hide what she was feeling. She wore her moods openly like the pearls that were always around her neck. If she was happy, it showed in the widest possible smile. Sadness was painted on her brow as it creased and puckered like a worn blouse. And dread showed in her eyes like deep black pools. That was what Henny saw now when she stared at her mother.

"Paul, what are they doing out on the water?"

Far shook his head. "I'm not sure. I thought perhaps this was just an exercise of some kind. But the men at the lighthouse seem to think differently."

"What are they saying?" Mor asked.

"Several boats have stopped by the lighthouse, and Nazi police have interrogated the men there. *Interrogated* is the word they used," Far explained. "The Nazis are asking a lot of questions about who comes by the lighthouse and who owns the boats that are on the water—that kind of thing. They even hinted that they might set up a command post at the lighthouse so they can watch what's going on even more closely. It's unnerved the men there."

"Is it possible that they're trying to take more control here, like they've done in other countries?" Mor asked.

"I don't want to jump to any conclusions," Far said. "But I certainly don't like the sight of them on the water, or at my lighthouse. And I don't like them asking a lot of questions!"

Henny frowned. "If it's only an exercise, then I wish they'd exercise somewhere else!"

At that, Mor dropped her hands and smiled weakly. "Agreed!" She waved her family toward the dining room table. "Okay, enough of that. Dinner is getting cold. It's time to eat."

Far turned on the radio on his way to the dining room, adjusting the dial until he had found a news report. It was a rare occurrence to have the radio on during family meals. It was usually the phonograph that was on in the background, mostly playing classical music, which Henny didn't mind. She had grown up listening to Beethoven, Brahms, Chopin, and others. She could tell a waltz from a minuet without having to ask. Far turned up the volume as the voice of a broadcaster boomed into the dining room.

"Really, Paul?" Mor asked. "It's dinnertime. I don't want to listen to politics when we're eating as a family."

"We can't ignore what's going on, my dear," Far replied. "Turning off the radio won't make these events go away."

Mor sighed as Henny moved closer to the radio. She, too, was curious about what was happening in her country. The broadcaster was reporting on the recent election in Denmark. Even though the Nazis had allowed the election to happen, the government of Nazi Germany was insisting that Denmark follow new rules: people could not assemble in public, strikes were outlawed, and anyone acting against the Nazis could face the death penalty. Henny thought of Otto's friend whose apartment had been searched after he'd attended a protest rally. She had heard about groups in Denmark that were banding together to try to disrupt the Nazis from gaining further control in her country. And even Far had mentioned that such a group had set fire to a building on the outskirts of the city. It was known to be a place where the Nazis had established offices. This threat of the death penalty was obviously a way to clamp down hard on activities like that.

On and on the report went. It ended with the voice of Adolf Hitler ranting, as he often did, about Jewish people—how evil they were, how they were the enemy of the state, how they were going to take over the world if they were not stopped. And he concluded with his vow to rid the world of every last one of them.

Henny had heard a lot of this before. And it always puzzled and disturbed her to hear Hitler talk wildly about all Jewish people as if they were less than human—insects, as he sometimes called them, needing to be crushed. Henny knew that in country after country across Europe, laws had stopped Jewish people from doing things that other citizens could do, like working, or owning businesses, or voting, or even shopping in stores or going to the movies. She also knew that Jewish people were being sent to terrible prisons where they were being tortured and killed. She shuddered at the thought. What was so wrong with being Jewish? It was simply a different religion. So what? The Rubin family were Jewish and had lived next door to Henny's family for years. The two families were friendly, often visiting one another. Henny had once gone with them to the Great Synagogue for a Sabbath service. The synagogue was a big brick building, more than 100 years old, with ornate pillars down its long aisles, wooden pews polished to a dark shine, and a gilded altar at the front. It was the first time Henny had ever been to a Jewish service. She didn't understand too much of it; most of it was conducted in the Hebrew language. But the songs were beautiful, bouncing and echoing off the walls and the towering vaulted ceiling. A couple of them reminded her of some classical pieces that she listened to on the radio. In that peaceful setting, Henny had felt as close to

God as she did in her own Lutheran church.

"This upsets me more than anything," Mor interrupted the broadcast. "The way Hitler talks about Jewish people—it's a disgrace."

"Thank goodness the Jews of Denmark are more respected," Far added.

That was true. The rights of Jewish citizens in Henny's country remained equal to the rest of the population. She hoped it would stay that way.

Mor looked up from the table as Hitler's tirade came to an end. "Have you heard enough?" she asked. "Can we turn it off now?"

Far nodded, and Henny moved over to switch off the radio. The silence that followed was welcome.

"What did you think you were going to hear?" asked Mor. "Hitler apologizing to the Jews?"

"He's a thug and a bully," Henny said.

Far looked troubled again. "I worry that he's more than that—worse than that."

"But those terrible things won't happen here, will they?" asked Henny. "I mean, Denmark isn't like all those other countries."

"I hope not, *min skat*," Far replied. He only called her "my treasure" when he was trying to make her feel better.

This time, his words didn't reassure her.

CHAPTER 3

After supper, Mor excused Henny from having to do the dishes—her usual job. Mor said she was looking forward to plunging her hands into soapy water and washing the dishes clean.

"Scrubbing the pots and pans will help rinse all those political thoughts out of my brain," Mor said. "You go outside and leave me on my own."

Henny walked out the back door and into a warm summer evening. She sat down on the lawn, looking out over the channel. The lights of the Drogden Lighthouse blinked on and off. Henny squinted into the distance. Sweden was out there, across the waterway. On a clear day, it sometimes looked so close that she thought she could swim over. On this dusky evening, she could barely make it out.

Once, Henny had sailed there with Far, when he had been asked to deliver some supplies to that country. The trip had taken a few hours, in water that had been so choppy and unpredictable that even Henny felt sick to her stomach—and she had always prided herself in being able to sail in any conditions. She had finally been forced to turn Gerda's wheel over to Far. She vowed that she would never do that trip ever again!

Other boats in the channel had also turned their lights on, twinkling like Christmas decorations out on the water. In the ever-darkening sky, it was impossible to see if any Nazi boats were out there among them, flying their flags. Henny still didn't understand what the Nazis were doing out there or why there were more of them than ever before. But, in this sea of flickering yellow lights, no one could tell an enemy boat apart from a Danish fisher or casual sailor. Henny liked it that way. She could believe that every boat on the water was a friendly one.

"What are you looking at?"

Henny startled out of her thoughts and turned to see her young neighbor, Susanne Rubin, standing over her, clutching firmly onto the hand of her two-year-old brother, Aron, who was pulling and tugging and obviously longing to get away.

Henny smiled warmly at Susanne. She had a special friendship with her young neighbor, much like an older sister to a younger one. After all, she had known Susanne from the time she was born, shortly after the Rubin family moved in next door. Henny had often helped look after Susanne when she was a baby. She had done the same when Aron came along. Now ten years old, Susanne had grown into a lively young girl with a wide, inviting smile and round curious eyes.

Susanne plunked herself down beside Henny and released her brother's hand. He wobbled unsteadily across the lawn. Then she snuggled up against Henny, curling her arm through Henny's like a vine. Despite their close friendship, Henny was sometimes still surprised that Susanne hugged her so easily. Mor and Far rarely hugged each other, let alone Henny. Not that they didn't love her; of course, they did. It just wasn't their way to be physically affectionate. They had taught Henny to greet strangers, friends, and even family members with a firm and respectful handshake.

"What are you looking at?" Susanne asked again.

"Just the lights out there."

"They're pretty."

"Yes, they are." Henny paused. "It's busy on the

channel tonight. Usually, I can count the lights. But tonight, there are too many."

Susanne lifted her hand and began counting the blinking lights, moving her finger across the channel as if she were following the words in a book. She gave up after reaching thirty. Watching her, Henny thought again about the Nazi boat they had seen earlier that day. And she thought about the news report with Hitler's angry attack against the Jews of Europe. How could someone as sweet as Susanne be considered evil? Henny wondered. But she knew that even children as young as Susanne and Aron were the targets of Hitler's rage.

"Why are the two of you still up?" Henny asked, not wanting to think about any of that, but focusing instead on her young friend.

"I can stay up as late as I want," Susanne said, rather defiantly.

Henny laughed. "When I was your age, I had to be in bed before the first street lamp came on."

Susanne's eyes widened. "You did? Not me. Aron is the one who should be in bed. But he couldn't sleep, so Mama said I should take him for a walk. I think she was hoping I'd make him tired. Plus, I think she needed the break."

Henny stifled a laugh. Susanne at the age of ten

was wise beyond her years.

"Mama says he can be quite difficult at times. Aron, come back here," she called out to her little brother, who had started to move toward the edge of the lawn.

Henny sat straighter. If Aron went much farther, he'd topple off the bank and into the channel.

"I'm not sure he's listening to you."

She made a move to stand and go after him when he suddenly turned toward the two of them, smiled impishly, and began to waddle back. He fell into Susanne's arms and giggled as she tickled him across his belly. Finally, he snuggled in between her legs and leaned his head back against her chest. Henny reached over and took his hand, opening it and tracing little circles around his palm. He grinned up at her. He had the same dark hair and round eyes as his sister.

"When are you going to take me sailing again?" Susanne suddenly asked. "I miss seeing Gerda."

Henny had taken Susanne out on the water a few months ago, and she took an instant liking to the sea. They'd gone a couple of times since, and now Susanne begged Henny to take her out again every time they saw each other.

"You said we could go another time. When?"

In addition to being mature for her age, Susanne

was bold. It was another thing that Henny liked about her.

"I'll take you soon," Henny replied, dropping Aron's hand and leaning back on her elbows.

"When?"

Henny smiled again. "You want a specific date?"

Susanne nodded.

"Okay," Henny replied, sitting back up. "Two days from now. I have to help my father do another run to the lighthouse. Ask one of your parents to bring you down to the pier, to where we park the *Gerda III*, and I'll take you out after I get back from that run. Gerda will be happy to see you," she added. "How does that sound?"

Just then, Susanne's mother poked her head out of the door of their house. "Hello, Henny," she called. "I hope Susanne isn't being a nuisance."

"Hi, Mrs. Rubin," Henny replied. "Don't worry about us. I love her company." The Rubins' house was an exact duplicate of Henny's, the same red-tiled roof, red shutters, and green door. In fact, Henny's entire neighborhood had homes that looked exactly alike.

Satisfied with Henny's response, Mrs. Rubin turned her attention to her daughter. "Susanne, is Aron asleep yet?"

When he heard his name, Aron sat up and

grinned in the direction of his mother. She sighed. "Okay, well I guess you should bring him back home and I'll deal with him." With that, she waved good-bye to Henny and closed the door.

Susanne stood up and lifted her brother into her arms. "Looks like we'll have another sleepless night," she said. "Blow a kiss to Henny, Aron."

Aron brought a pudgy hand up to his mouth and then flung it away in Henny's direction. She smiled and waved back at him.

"I'll see you in two days. Right, Henny?" Susanne asked.

Mrs. Rubin's head appeared once more in their doorway, calling out again for Susanne to come back in with Aron. But Susanne ignored her, looking eagerly at Henny.

"Right?" she asked again.

Henny smiled up at her. "I promise."

CHAPTER 4

The next morning, Henny overslept, setting off late for her mile-long walk to school. Last night's radio report about the Nazis and Hitler had played over and over in her mind, like one of Far's records when it skipped and got stuck in a loop on the phonograph. Between that, the Nazi boat sighting, and thoughts of Susanne somehow caught in the middle of it all, she'd had a very hard time falling asleep.

Up ahead, she could see her friends leaning against the school building, waiting for the bell to ring. She joined them, exchanging greetings with everyone. Lukas made room for her beside him. "You're late," he said, smiling down at her.

Lukas was tall for his sixteen years, with blond hair that flopped down like a mop on his forehead, covering his eyes. When their teacher, Mr. Jepsen, wasn't telling Lukas to get a haircut, he was scolding him for letting his shirttail hang out of his trousers. Even when Lukas managed to tuck in the shirt, it would somehow find a way out, as if, like his hair, it had a mind of its own. So far, Lukas had resisted the strong suggestion that he cut his hair. He flipped his bangs aside, but a second later, they crept back over his face. Henny liked that Lukas pushed the limits of acceptable appearance in school. It made him interesting and a bit daring.

"I slept in," Henny replied.

"Did you study for the test?"

That question came from Emma, standing with her twin sister, Sophia. The twins were identical in every way, the same deep-blue eyes and the same bright-red, curly hair, always worn in the same style, pulled over to one side and held in place with identical hair clips. They even stood the same way, their heads titled slightly to the right when someone was speaking, as if that helped them to listen. The only way to tell them apart was that Emma wore glasses and Sophia didn't.

Henny shrugged. School had never been her strength. She managed to get through most of her subjects with average grades, but she found it all so boring! She would rather be out sailing than sitting in a classroom listening to her teacher drone on about literature or mathematics. She was going to follow in her father's footsteps and join the navy, so what did it matter if she was good in those subjects, or any subject. She could steer a boat out of a narrow channel practically with her eyes closed. She could sense when the winds had changed and bad weather was moving in. She had told all of this to Far, but he had been unimpressed.

"And do you think I became a naval officer because I didn't pay attention in school?" he asked. "It's my studies in mathematics and geography and science that got me to this position."

Henny knew in her heart that what her father said was true. If only her classroom could be on the sea, especially at this time of year when the weather was so hot. The school year for all Danish children began in early August. A classroom on the sea would have been so much more interesting. It would have made everything make more sense!

"We studied," the twins said in unison, speaking almost as one person, which they often did. Emma had once told Henny that she and her sister felt a sort of whispering in their heads that made them know what the other was thinking or feeling or even about to say. It was as if they shared the same mind. That fascinated Henny, though she couldn't imagine being that connected to another person.

"I'm ready," Lukas added easily. He was a top-notch student and aced every test, which was probably the reason Mr. Jepsen didn't press him more firmly to cut his hair or fix his careless appearance.

"I'll bet you didn't even open a book," Henny said. It sometimes infuriated her that some people, like Lukas, found school so easy when she struggled most days. "And what about you?" she asked Erik, who stood with them by the school wall.

If Lukas was considered casual or even sloppy in appearance, then Erik was the complete opposite. He was always neatly dressed, shoes polished, his dark hair short and straight, with a razor-sharp part on one side. Erik was one of the quietest kids in school—the kind who watched what was going on but said little. Henny and Erik had been closer when they were younger and conversation had been less important than just playing together. They had drifted apart since then.

"Are you ready for the test?" Henny asked Erik again. She wanted to try to include him in the conversation.

He shrugged. "I'll be okay."

Erik's family had come from Germany when he was a little boy, which had never really mattered to Henny one way or the other. But now, with Germany at the center of everything happening in the world these days, she wondered what Erik thought about it all. She knew better than to ask, though. Even if he did have opinions about it, it would be like pulling teeth to get him to talk. She turned away and gazed out past the schoolyard to the field that the high school shared with the elementary school. Sure enough, she spotted Susanne playing in the field. At that moment, Susanne looked up, saw Henny, and waved. Henny smiled and waved back. Then, Susanne mimed sailing a boat, hands on an imaginary steering wheel, turning it quickly to the left and then to the right. Henny smiled again and gave her a thumbs-up.

When Henny turned back to her group, Erik was staring at her, his dark eyes probing. An uneasy feeling passed through her. No reason for that, she thought. Still, she shook her arms, as if she was shaking the feeling away just as the bell rang and students began to gather their bags and join the line to enter the school building. Erik turned and moved to the door.

"Good luck on the test," the twins declared.

Henny waited while Lukas bent to retrieve his book bag. The bag was open, and while he was trying to get it closed, a couple of papers from inside fell out. Henny gasped when she saw what was printed on them. Each sheet had a swastika printed at the top. But the hated symbol had a thick, black X drawn across it.

Henny had just managed to get that horrible image out of her head, and here it was again, following her around like a mosquito. Lukas looked up and saw her face. He reddened.

"Lukas, what are you doing with those papers?" Henny's voice shook. With all the recent talk of severe punishment for anyone speaking out against the Nazis, seeing these pamphlets unnerved her more than ever.

He grabbed the sheets and shoved them into his bag. "It's nothing."

"But those Nazi signs! Why are you carrying them around?"

Lukas closed his bag tightly and stood. "I said it's nothing. Good luck on the test, Henny."

And before Henny could say another word, Lukas bolted for the school building, leaving her standing there, all alone.

CHAPTER 5

The next day, Henny was steering the *Gerda III* to her berth in Copenhagen after a run to the lighthouse with Far. The air was warm. The sky was clear and beginning to turn a colorful mix of blue tinged with red as the sun was just starting to go down. It would be a good evening to take Susanne out for a sail, as Henny had promised.

Far looked calm, kidding with Henny the way he usually did when he was in a good mood and things were going well. He even started telling jokes.

"How many apples grow on a tree?" Far asked.

Henny groaned and rolled her eyes even before hearing the answer. Far's jokes were hardly ever funny.

"All of them!" Far declared.

"Good one, sir," Otto said, turning to grin at Henny. "And what does a clock do when it's hungry?" Far continued.

Henny hoped this would be the last one.

"It goes back *four* seconds. Do you get it?" Far asked. "Not FOR seconds, but FOUR seconds!" He held four fingers up in the air.

"I get it," Henny said. Far grinned from ear to ear. Henny couldn't get the boat back to shore fast enough.

As they approached the pier, she could see Susanne waiting for her, impatiently shifting from one foot to the other, then bouncing up on her toes like a sprinter about to take off on a race. Her father stood beside her, clutching her hand as if he were holding her back.

Far put his hand on Henny's arm.

"Otto and Gerhardt must go with you when you go out again," he said.

"But why?" Henny protested. She often took Gerda out on her own. She didn't need Otto and Gerhardt watching over her, or babysitting her, or whatever it was that Far thought they had to do. She wasn't a child, and she didn't like it when Far treated her like one.

Was he still thinking about Nazi boats on the

channel? There hadn't been any today—at least none that Henny could see. Their delivery of supplies to the lighthouse had gone smoothly. The channel had been as calm and peaceful as Henny had always known it to be.

"We didn't see any swastikas today, Far," Henny said. "Are you worried about that? Is that why you want Otto and Gerhardt to go with me?"

If Far was thinking about the Nazis, he wasn't saying. Instead, he pointed at Susanne on the pier, bouncing up and down like a rubber ball while her father still held firmly to her hand. Susanne looked like she might fly off the dock if he let go. "You might need some help with that little girl while she's on board. Safety first! That's what's most important, isn't it, Henny?" Far said, looking straight into Henny's eyes.

Henny lowered her head. "Yes, Far." It did no good to try and argue with him when he looked at her that way. Besides, it didn't really matter one way or the other if Otto and Gerhardt went along, she reasoned. She was still the one in charge of the outing.

Carefully, she eased the boat up to the dock while Otto and Gerhardt jumped off, ropes in hand, waiting to steady Gerda so that Susanne could climb on board. Far descended onto the pier and walked over to shake hands with Mr. Rubin.

"Nice to see you, Victor," Far said, greeting their neighbor.

"It's good to see you too, Paul. I left my office early today so that I could bring Susanne down to the pier."

Mr. Rubin worked as a lawyer. Far had often told Henny that Mr. Rubin's busy practice meant that he came home late at night most days. He even worked on weekends. "I hope it isn't too much trouble for Henny to give Susanne a ride."

"No trouble at all. I know how much Henny enjoys spending time with your daughter." Far bent toward Susanne and reached out to shake her hand, as well. "Hello, Miss Rubin. Are you looking forward to a boat ride?"

Susanne accepted the outstretched hand and then curtsied. "Oh, yes, Mr. Sinding. Henny said she might let me steer today."

"My hands will be on the wheel, as well," Henny called out from on board. "You forgot to add that part, Susanne." All Henny needed was for Far to think she was going to let Susanne sail Gerda on her own. He might never let her take the boat out again if that were the case—with or without Otto and Gerhardt!

Susanne's face reddened. "I meant that you said I

could *help* steer. That's what I meant."

"You'll make a fine first mate," Far said, straightening. "Henny can teach you everything you need to know about sailing."

"I'll walk Susanne home after our boat ride, Mr. Rubin," Henny said. "You don't need to wait for her." Henny was eager to get going. If they waited much longer, the sun would be setting and their ride would be cut short. Besides, Susanne looked as if she might explode if they didn't get the boat out onto the water soon!

Otto and Gerhardt helped Susanne onto Gerda and then jumped on after her. She stood next to Henny by the gunnels, and together they waved to Mr. Rubin and Far. Henny watched the two men turn to walk back to their homes, heads bent together, probably discussing politics, Henny assumed. She guided Susanne up to the bow of the boat, instructing her to hold on to one of the masts while she returned to the wheel inside the little cabin and began to steer Gerda out into the channel. Otto stood close to Susanne at the bow. *Safety first*, Henny thought, echoing Far's words in her mind. But she needn't have worried. As the boat bobbed and weaved out of the harbor, all the restless energy that Henny had witnessed in Susanne while she stood on shore seemed to ebb out of her. She stood in one spot, holding tightly onto the mast. Her face was turned toward the sun, which was beginning to set on the horizon. Her long, dark hair blew off her shoulders and straight back behind her. Otto turned and gave Henny a thumbs-up and Henny revved the motor to pick up speed. Susanne squealed with delight, clutching the mast even tighter.

Once they were in the middle of the channel, Henny cut the motor and instructed Otto and Gerhardt to raise Gerda's sails. The two men untied the main mast from its support anchors. Once they had checked all of the connections, they began to pull on the line, hand over hand, hoisting the mainsail until it swelled in the wind. Then, they cleated the mainsail and moved to raise the two smaller sails. It was as if a flower had opened its petals. That's what Henny always thought when the sails were raised. It was the part she loved most. She began to steer Gerda upwind, letting the wind fill the sails even more and taking the boat farther and farther into the channel. Gerda bounced on the waves, sending a cold spray onto the deck. At the front, Susanne squealed again.

"Hang on," Henny called out.

Susanne turned back to Henny, grinning like someone had just handed her the present she had been waiting for her entire life. Henny's heart swelled when she saw Susanne's face. That feeling of joy was exactly what Henny experienced every time she was out on the water and the sails had been raised, no sounds except for the rushing wind, the splash of waves, and the cry of seagulls above her. It was heaven.

After a few minutes of sailing, Henny called out again to Susanne. "Come back here to the helm so that you can steer with me."

Otto escorted the little girl to the small cabin and Henny moved over to make room for Susanne to stand behind the wheel. "Picture the face of a clock. Your left hand goes on the ten and your right hand at about two o'clock. Here and here." She lifted Susanne's hands up to the steering wheel.

Susanne stood on her tiptoes. "I can't see anything," she said.

Henny looked around. Gerhardt suddenly appeared carrying a small box. "This might help," he said, placing the box on the floor just in front of Susanne. "Henny used to stand on this when she was even smaller than you. Do you remember that, Henny?"

Henny smiled as the memory crept up on her. "Of course, I do. You're the one who taught me where to place my hands on the wheel as well."

"It worked for Henny and it'll work for you. Jump on up, little lady," Gerhardt said reaching out to give Susanne a hand.

Susanne stepped onto the box and once again reached up to take the wheel. "Ten o'clock and two o'clock," she muttered, placing her hands in the correct positions.

Henny wrapped her hands around Susanne's, helping guide the boat through the waves and then turning it to tack in the opposite direction, back and forth, keeping the wind in the sails and the boat moving at a brisk clip.

"You've got it!" Henny exclaimed, feeling Susanne exert more pressure on the wheel as if she was beginning to understand how the wind worked and how she could steer the boat forward. "I think that Gerda likes you. She's responding easily. She doesn't do that for every sailor."

"That's silly," Susanne said. "This is just a boat. It doesn't know who I am."

"First of all, Gerda is a *she*, not an *it*. And secondly, you're wrong. She may be a boat, but she can tell who's at the wheel and whether or not that person feels confident or is afraid. Isn't that right, Gerda?"

Susanne moved her head forward as if she were

listening for something. Her face was alive and eager. The wind blowing past her ears was the only response. Susanne frowned. "SHE didn't say anything."

"Oh, she doesn't talk. That's not what I meant. But you can tell by how easily she moves that she heard me. That's her way of answering. You must be feeling very confident for Gerda to move like this."

In response, Susanne gripped the wheel tighter, leaned forward, and pulled her shoulders back. Henny deliberately turned the boat into the wind, letting it pick up even more speed until it was practically flying over the waves.

Susanne grinned. "I hear her," she shouted.

Together they stood at the helm, steering in one direction and then in the other, weaving back and forth as if they were dancing on the water. No other boats were around. It felt as if they owned the channel. Henny was just about to tack in the opposite direction one more time when she suddenly spied a lone boat in the distance moving in their direction. She stiffened and her stomach plunged when she saw the dreaded swastika flag flying from its mast.

Otto and Gerhardt appeared in the cabin to stand next to her. Clearly, they had seen the boat as well. They didn't look nearly as shocked as Henny felt.

"Your father was afraid this might happen," Otto

whispered in Henny's ear, not wanting Susanne to hear.

So, Far *had* been worried, Henny realized.

"Lousy Nazis are at it again," Otto said. "They arrested my friend, the one I told you about who had his apartment searched. I have no idea where they've taken him, or why! But I'm worried sick."

"If I could ever find a way to stand up to those thugs, I'd grab it in a heartbeat," Gerhardt added.

"Me too!" said Otto. "Why don't they just get out of this country and leave us alone. We don't want them here."

"We don't want them anywhere!" said Gerhardt.

Henny's heart was racing. She couldn't believe this was happening again, and especially on this perfect day, and with Susanne on the boat. Susanne didn't seem to have noticed a thing. She still happily clutched the wheel, helping Henny guide Gerda across the water.

"I think it's time we head for home," Henny said, raising her voice to be heard above the wind, one eye out in the distance, watching the Nazi boat. She wasn't sure what it was that she was so afraid of. She hadn't done anything wrong; she had every right to be out on the channel. But still, all the recent talk about the Nazis increasing their presence in the city and on the water; it was all unsettling. Not to mention the arrest of Otto's friend. All she knew was that she didn't want that boat anywhere near her—or near Susanne.

"No, not yet," Susanne protested. "We've hardly had any time out here."

"We'll come out another day. I promise. But for now, I think I need to get you home. Lower the sails," she instructed Otto and Gerhardt, before Susanne could say another word.

Once the men had brought the sails down, tying them onto the masts, they gave Henny a sign that she could move. Henny turned the key in the ignition and brought the motor to life, helping Susanne jump off the small box and stand next to her. Then, she turned the boat around and began to drive it back to shore. She glanced over her shoulder. The Nazi boat had changed direction and was moving back across the channel. Henny let out her breath.

Susanne tugged on Henny's arm. "Is it that boat? Is that why we're going back so soon?"

So, Susanne had noticed after all! "Do you understand who's on that boat?" Henny asked.

Susanne nodded, looking thoughtful. "I know they don't like Jewish people at all. Mama and Papa talk about what's happening to Jews in other countries.

But then, they just get sad and stop. My aunt Agata and uncle Samuel live in Poland. We used to get letters from them all the time. But not anymore."

Henny gulped. "We're all lucky to be living here in Denmark and not somewhere else."

Susanne stood quietly as Henny approached the pier and eased Gerda into its berth. Otto and Gerhardt jumped onto the dock to secure the boat.

"I'm sorry the ride was short," Henny said to Susanne when she had helped her off the boat and was standing beside her on shore.

Susanne smiled weakly. "That's okay." Her voice was unconvincing. "And I really want to thank you for taking me out today."

Henny lifted Susanne's chin so that their eyes met. "We'll do it again, another day. I promise. And I'll let you hold the steering wheel, just like you did today. Would you like that?"

Susanne threw her arms around Henny's neck, squeezing tightly. "Oh yes," she cried. "I want to learn as much as I can. I want to be a sailor, just like you!"

Henny released Susanne's grip, took her hand, and together they began to walk home.

CHAPTER 6

Too many swastikas, Henny thought: on the boats in the channel and on the papers that had fallen out of Lukas's book bag. After her boat ride with Susanne, Far had tried to reassure Henny that the Nazis wouldn't go any further than patrolling the waterway. But she was unconvinced and so disheartened by it all.

The next morning at school, she was determined to corner Lukas and ask him about those papers with the crossed-out swastikas. Maybe he would be able to help her make sense of everything. She had tried to ask him about it when she had seen the papers fall out of his bag. Instead, he had wished her luck on that dreaded mathematics test. Questions about her schoolwork always flustered her, and he knew it. Since then, he had been avoiding her. But now she felt more strongly that she had to get some information from him. He couldn't avoid her forever.

Henny cornered him in the schoolyard before classes. She wasted no time.

"I saw those papers in your bag, Lukas. Something's going on. What is it?" He made a move to walk past her, but she stepped sideways to block his path. "Please talk to me. What were those papers?"

"They're nothing," Lukas replied, brushing his mop of hair out of his eyes. "They're just some stupid flyers that were in my bag."

"But I saw the symbol on them." Henny glanced around and then lowered her voice. "The swastika."

Lukas also looked around. The two of them stood at their usual spot by the school wall. Their friends were gathered together across the field. The twins were there, talking in unison, their arms narrating a story in identical rhythm. Henny waited, watching silently as Lukas squirmed, brushed his hair back off his face again, and sighed.

"How much do you know about what's happening with our country and Nazi Germany?" he finally asked.

"I know enough," Henny replied. "I know that we've always resisted being drawn under the Nazis' spell. I know that King Christian is a strong leader and wants to keep Denmark independent." Everybody knew this. What did it have to do with the papers in Lukas's bag?

Lukas bent toward her. "Things are getting worse, Henny. I'm not sure King Christian is going to be able to resist for much longer."

Henny's eyes widened. Far had said that as long as the king was in power, everything would be fine. Lukas was suggesting that the protection from their king was about to disappear. She told him about the boats out on the channel flying the Nazi flag.

"That may just be the start of what's to come. I've heard that the Nazis may step in and dissolve our government," Lukas said. "Throw King Christian out and place their own military in power."

Henny gasped. "But we'd never let that happen."

"We may not have a choice." Lukas glanced around and then lowered his voice. "That's what those papers are all about. There are groups of us who are trying to stop the Nazis. Not by fighting—at least not yet. But we're protesting against them, and spying on them. We're part of the Danish Resistance. We're passing out pamphlets—like the papers you saw in my bag—ones that describe how evil the Nazis are and how we need to resist their demands. Last week, we snuck into a building where a unit of Nazi soldiers had set up a command post. It was late at night when no one was around. We stole a bunch of their files and mixed up the papers that were there in their cabinets." Lukas smiled proudly. "It's going to take them weeks to figure out what their orders are."

Henny's head was spinning. This was not what she had expected Lukas to say—not what she thought he was doing. She had wanted reassurances from him that everything was fine, that the Nazi symbols on his paper were unimportant, that he wasn't doing anything to get himself in trouble. Instead, he was saying that the Nazis were becoming more powerful in Denmark and that he was right in the middle of trying to interfere with their activities. She never imagined that he would be capable of taking such risks. The building that had been set on fire last week—the one Far had told her about—had Lukas been part of that? "But how did you get involved with all this?" she asked.

"There are groups all across the country that all have the same goal: to resist the Nazi occupation of our country. I asked around and found someone who introduced me to one of the groups here in Copenhagen. That's how I got in." He glanced around again. "I don't want to say much more than that. We have to be careful."

Henny listened with a sensation of fear rising in her stomach. "But it all sounds so dangerous. Did you hear the latest warning? Danish citizens could get the death penalty if they're caught in acts of sabotage against the Nazis. Doesn't that scare you?"

Lukas shrugged. "Let them try and stop us." Then, his face became serious. "Of course, it's dangerous. But we can't keep our heads in the sand, Henny. We need to come together as one voice against them— show them that we won't bend to their rules like other countries have." Lukas flipped his hair off his eyes again. "I know you're friends with that Jewish girl who goes to the elementary school. Do you know what the Nazis are doing to Jews in other countries?"

Of course, she knew. Those reports were even more terrifying than the voice of Hitler himself. "That could never happen here," Henny declared.

"What makes you think it can't? Don't be naive, Henny. The Nazis are powerful and Denmark is a tiny country. They'll swallow us up if we don't do something."

She didn't believe him. She didn't want to believe him. But then, why did she race back to shore yesterday when she saw the Nazi boat? She felt so confused!

Henny stared at her friend. "I'm worried about you, Lukas—about what you're doing." She couldn't even think about the possibility that he might be arrested for his activities—that he might be killed.

Lukas smiled. "Then I guess we can't let them catch us." He took a step toward her, his eyes lighting up. "Henny, haven't you ever thought about speaking out against the Nazis and what they're doing in our country?"

"Me? Why ... no ... I haven't thought about ..." She stopped. All of this was still so new to her: the increased presence of the Nazis in Denmark, the new laws aimed at stopping those who opposed them, the threat to Jews in her country. Of course, she hated everything that was happening. But actually helping fight the Nazis was another story.

Lukas pulled back and his face grew somber again. "Look, I've told you things that you can't repeat to anyone—not to your parents or anyone you know. I trust you, Henny. But it's hard to know these days who is a friend and who isn't."

"Of course," Henny replied, nodding. "I won't say a word. Just be careful, Lukas. Promise me that."

Lukas smiled again. He shifted his bag to his other shoulder and the two of them began to walk around the building. Turning the corner, they nearly ran headlong into Erik. Henny glanced back at Lukas, who had bent down to tie his shoelace. How long had

Erik been standing there? she wondered nervously. Had he overheard their conversation? And what if he had? Everything that Lukas was doing was risky—to himself and to the others with whom he was involved. He had said it was hard to know who to trust. If Erik had overheard, was he trustworthy?

"Hi, Erik," Henny said, trying to keep her voice as light and even as she could.

Erik's eyes darted quickly from Lukas to Henny. Did he know something? Meanwhile, Lukas didn't say a word. He stood calmly beside Henny, shifting his book bag from one shoulder to the other.

Just then, the piercing ring of the school bell echoed through the yard. The timing couldn't have been better. Lukas grabbed Henny by the arm and pulled her forward. She could feel her arm shaking beneath his, and her face felt hot. Before entering the building, Lukas leaned toward her.

"Relax. I don't think he heard anything."

Henny wished she felt as confident as Lukas sounded.

Chapter 7

As soon as the bell rang at the end of the day, Henny bolted out the school doors. She had felt distracted all day, glancing at Erik for any sign that he was watching her or Lukas. But there didn't appear to be a shift in Erik's behavior. He kept to himself and was as quiet as always.

As she made her way home, her mind was reeling. Lukas! Her head throbbed with all the information that he had shared with her. A resistance movement in Copenhagen! People trying to rise up against the Nazis in any way they could. And Lukas in the middle of it all! The work he was doing sounded incredibly dangerous, and it was—especially given the recent ruling about a death penalty to those who would oppose the Nazis.

On top of all of that, if what Lukas had told her was true—that the Nazis were stepping up their efforts to take over Denmark—then Jews in Copenhagen would be in great danger, people like Susanne and her family and all the other Jewish families who lived here. Someone needed to stop the Nazis. And maybe if Lukas was courageous enough to be part of a group that was trying to do just that, then good for him! And good for all those like him who were part of the Resistance. But did she have it in her to join them?

One minute, Henny's head pounded with fears for Lukas, and for Susanne! And the next, she was cheering Lukas and others who were trying to oppose the Nazis. It was as if a swarm of bees had taken up residence in her brain and were buzzing around in there with an intensity that she hadn't ever felt in her life.

She wound her way through the streets of her city toward her home, passing the shops and merchants she had passed every day for years. Nothing seemed different. Everyone was going about their business. Shopkeepers invited passersby to come in and sample their wares. Men zigzagged through the crowds of people, anxious to get home from work. A mother pulled on the hand of her toddler while struggling under the weight of a grocery bag. A little girl bounced a ball against the wall of a building until the owner came outside and shooed her away. How could anything be so wrong in her country when everything seemed so fine, so normal?

She rounded a corner and came to a sudden stop. Up ahead, two Nazi soldiers were standing with their backs to her. They were dressed in gray uniforms with that ugly swastika emblazoned on their armbands. Henny froze, dread surging through her. She knew that she should probably give these soldiers as wide a berth as possible, as she had done the couple of times she'd seen them before, as she did out on the water with Gerda. But there was a crowd gathering around the soldiers, and her curiosity outweighed her fear. As she peered over the heads of the people who had rushed in front of her, she could see an elderly man cowering in front of the soldiers. He was Jewish. She knew that from the skullcap that was perched on his head, knocked slightly to one side when one of the soldiers grabbed him roughly by the arm. The second soldier gripped his other arm, and together, they began to pull him down the street toward a truck parked at the end of the block.

"No! Please don't take me," the man cried out. "My family! My children! What will they think? How will they manage without me?"

Henny's face burned with anger, and her heart

raced. She searched the crowd of people around her. Was there anyone who would be able to help this poor man? No one moved.

"You should have thought of that before you started passing out these," one soldier replied, shoving a sheet of paper in the man's face. From Henny's vantage point, the paper looked very much like the kind of flyer she had seen in Lukas's bag.

"But it wasn't me," the man protested. "I didn't do anything wrong."

"We don't believe you," the second soldier said. "Besides, you'll be one less Jew on the streets of Copenhagen. There are too many of you anyway— here and everywhere else."

The soldiers reached the truck and lifted the man off his feet, depositing him into the truck's open back as if he were a sack of garbage.

Just then, a young man standing behind Henny pushed past everyone and came to stand in front of the Nazi soldiers. "Stop treating him like that," the man said, hands on his hips, feet apart. "He says he hasn't done anything wrong."

This young man didn't appear to be that much older than Henny. She held her breath. Would the soldiers believe him? Would they back down and release the man in the truck? Henny looked up. The

Jewish man was standing in the truck bed, eyes closed, hands clasped in front of him as if he were praying. The soldiers paused, looking the young man up and down. Then, they both reached out at the same moment and grabbed him on either side.

"You think you can speak to us that way?" one soldier cried.

"Well, maybe you should just join your friend," the other said. "You'll both see what happens when you oppose us."

With that, the soldiers hoisted the young man up into the air and threw him in the truck. He hit the floor with a thud and didn't move. Then the soldiers turned to face the crowd, which had grown silent and still.

"A saboteur was hanged today for speaking out against us," one soldier said. "Maybe these two will be next. Let this be a warning to all of you. You cannot stop us, and you cannot go against us. So don't try!"

Then, the soldiers got into the truck, revved its motor, and drove it away, turning a corner and disappearing from view. All that was left was a puff of black smoke from the truck's exhaust. And that too disappeared within seconds.

Henny's heart was pounding so hard she was certain that those around her could hear it. She clutched at her chest and turned once more to face the people in the crowd, desperate for someone to acknowledge that what she had just witnessed wasn't an illusion. Everyone looked stunned. But no one would meet her gaze.

A moment later, the crowd began to disperse. Shopkeepers moved into their stores. Men and women pushed past her as if they couldn't get away from the scene fast enough. The little girl who had bounced her ball against the wall of that building was sitting on the curb, head lowered, rocking back and forth.

Henny looked around. The street where something so shocking and terrible had just happened was now nearly deserted. It was as though nothing had happened at all.

She turned and ran. She didn't stop until she reached home.

CHAPTER 8

Thankfully, Mor and Far were there, seated at the dining room table, sipping tea as they often did at the end of the day. Henny threw herself into a chair next to Mor and recounted everything she had seen on the street—the Nazi soldiers, the Jewish man tossed into the truck, the young man who had tried to help, and the crowd of people, all dumbfounded by what they had witnessed. Far's face grew pale as Henny spoke. Mor clasped her hands together so tightly that her knuckles turned white, and she lowered her head. Her face said it all.

"Where do you think the soldiers took those men?" Henny asked. "And what's going to happen to them?"

Far seemed to ignore the question. His eyes were down. "I knew things were getting worse," he said. "I just didn't think it would happen so fast."

"What do you mean 'getting worse'?"

He looked up. "Those boats that we've seen on the water, Henny, and now these soldiers arresting people. Our country has resisted the Nazis for so long. But I fear that we can't stand up to them for much longer."

Lukas was right! She hadn't wanted to believe it was possible. But Far was saying the same thing. And after what she'd witnessed on the street today, she knew in her heart that all this was true.

Mor lifted her head. "I've heard there are groups of resisters that have sprung up across the city and in other cities around the country," she said. "People who are trying to stop the Nazis from taking over Denmark."

There was a throbbing in Henny's chest that was rising up into her neck and into her ears. Her head was beginning to feel light. Lukas was part of that resistance. He had told her all about their activities. She bit her teeth into her lower lip. Oh, how she longed to tell Far and Mor about Lukas. But she had promised him she wouldn't say a word. And she couldn't betray that trust—not even to her parents.

"Those men and women who are standing up to the Nazis," Far continued. "They're so incredibly brave, despite the risks they're taking."

"I know," Henny whispered. "The death penalty."

"Yes," Far replied. "It's dangerous, and still they plow forward. I admire each and every one of them. If anyone can save our country, it's them."

Daring and brave. That was the combination it would take to be a part of a group willing to stand up to the Nazis. Thank goodness for people like Lukas, Henny thought. He had those qualities. Others did as well. She wondered again if she might have those qualities too. Did she have what it would take to be part of their group—to swallow her fear and fight for what she knew to be right? An idea was running through Henny's mind, a plan that would require her to be daring and brave as well. She wasn't sure about it yet, wasn't sure how or what she could do. And the thought of being arrested, or worse, shook her to the core. But adrenaline was coursing through her body. And after what she had witnessed on the streets of Copenhagen today, and after all that she was hearing about the rising tension in her country, maybe it was time to put herself on the line.

Over dinner, her parents continued to talk about the rising Nazi presence and the work of the resisters, as well as the Jewish families in Denmark who would be at even greater risk if the Nazis took over. Henny listened in silence. At one point, Far looked at her.

"Are we frightening you, Henny, with all this political talk?"

She shook her head. "I need to understand everything that's happening—I *want* to understand."

Far nodded and he and Mor continued to talk. After dinner, Henny helped her mother clean up, and then she excused herself and went out into the backyard. She sank into the grass, staring out at the channel that had always been her safe place. Now, with those Nazi boats out there, it didn't *feel* safe. Tonight, though, the channel looked peaceful again. Lights were blinking, a soft breeze was blowing, and stars dotted the sky like a painting. Henny leaned her head back and closed her eyes.

"What are you thinking about?"

Susanne really knew how to sneak up on her! Henny opened her eyes and smiled at her young friend. "Can't Aron sleep again?" she asked, sitting up and looking around for the little boy.

"Oh, he's fast asleep," Susanne replied. "I just came out to see if you were around. And here you are."

Susanne plunked herself down in the grass next to Henny and leaned against her. "You looked like you were thinking about something very important."

How could Henny even begin to explain to Susanne all the worries that were parading through her mind? "I was just thinking about school," she said, instead. "I had a mathematics test earlier this week, and I'm afraid I didn't do very well." It wasn't really a lie.

Susanne looked up at her. "I do very well in mathematics," she said, sounding more like a grown-up than a ten-year-old. "Do you want me to help you?"

Henny laughed, the first one in a long time. "I wish you could, Susanne. But I think what I'm supposed to be learning in mathematics and what you're learning are two very different things."

Susanne nodded. "I just thought ... I thought if I helped you out, maybe you'd take me sailing again." She bit her lower lip and looked away.

Henny nudged her friend playfully. "I promised I'd take you out on the water again, and I will. You don't need to offer me anything in return. It makes me happy that you enjoy sailing as much as I do."

Susanne settled back against Henny. "I want to be just like you when I grow up."

This simple and innocent wish caught Henny off guard. She blinked, trying to stop the tears that suddenly gathered behind her eyes. The two sat in silence for a few more minutes until Susanne's mother appeared at their back door. "It's getting late, Susanne," she called out to her. "How are you, Henny?" she added.

"I'm well, thank you, Mrs. Rubin," Henny answered. "Susanne and I were just talking about sailing."

"She talks of little else! But now, it's time to come in."

As Susanne stood, Henny reached out to grab her hand. "I hope you're being careful out on the streets these days." Henny didn't want to scare the young girl, but after what she'd witnessed this afternoon, she feared for her friend's safety.

Susanne nodded solemnly. "I know. My parents are saying the same thing. Don't worry, Henny," she added. "I'm very grown-up for my age."

Henny felt too sad to speak. She could only nod, and watch Susanne walk back toward her house.

The next day, Henny found Lukas alone in the school-yard. "I want to help," she said.

She had barely slept the night before. Between her earlier conversation with Lukas, the terrible incident she'd witnessed on the street when the two men were arrested, and then hearing Susanne's childlike statement about being grown-up, something in Henny had changed. She needed to do something, to stand up to those who would overrun her country, who would hurt her neighbors, her fellow Danes. Her feelings scared her—terrified her, in fact! Who wouldn't be afraid to stand up to the Nazis? But she couldn't sit still and do nothing. *Daring and brave.* Those were the words that kept playing in her mind as she faced Lukas in the schoolyard.

"Help with what?" he asked, flipping his bangs off his face.

Henny glanced around. The field appeared to be deserted, but it didn't hurt to check and make sure no one was lurking about. "I want to join up with your resisters, or whatever your group is called. I want to be part of it."

Lukas looked around as well, and then took Henny's arm. He stepped closer to her and bent forward until they were face to face. "Do you understand what you're saying? This isn't a game, Henny. What we're doing is important work. You said you'd never thought about doing anything like this before. So why the change of heart?"

Henny swallowed hard. She told Lukas about the arrest of the two men on the street. "You said that we can't keep our heads in the sand. And I realized that you're right. I want to help. I want to be part of any group that stands up to the Nazis."

Lukas was silent, staring at Henny, appearing to think and rethink what she had said, just as she had pondered the risks and gains of asking to join him.

"Let me come with you," Henny said. "Please!"

More seconds passed. Finally, Lukas stood back and breathed in deeply. "All right," he said. "Give me a couple of days. And remember, you can't tell your parents about this. No one can know."

CHAPTER 9

Several days later, Lukas came up to her in the schoolyard.

"Tonight," he said, lowering his voice. "Meet me at ten o'clock, outside the train station, in front of the big clock. Can you be there?"

Ten o'clock was late. This was going to be tricky, but Henny knew she would find a way. There was no turning back now. She nodded.

"And wear something dark," he added. "We're going to be out on the streets."

She told her parents that she was going to study at the twins' house. She would be back very late, and they shouldn't wait up for her, she said. Her parents accepted this with no questions asked. In fact, they seemed pleased that Henny was devoting an evening to her studies. She hated having to lie to them—it was something she hadn't done in the past. But in her heart, she knew they would understand the importance of what she was about to do. Hadn't Far said that he admired anyone who would be part of the resistance? He had said that the resisters would be the ones to save their country. This lie was necessary, she told herself as she slipped out of the house.

She walked to a café in the center of the city, one that she knew would stay open late. She stayed there, nervously sipping tea, and then ran to their meeting spot just as the clock tower bells were chiming ten. Lukas was waiting for her.

He didn't waste any time. Without a word, he took off, leading Henny on a twisting journey through the streets of Copenhagen, turning this way and that until she had completely lost her bearings. It was a struggle to keep up with him in the darkness. Her eyes remained glued to the back of his head—his blond hair reflecting the only bit of light on an otherwise pitch-black evening. She was terrified she might lose sight of him, and then what would she do? She had no idea where she was. There weren't even any stars out to help light her path. And the moon had disappeared behind some clouds, leaving only its ghostly outline in the sky.

On and on they went, zigzagging around a maze
of buildings and through narrow alleys. Henny stayed
as close to Lukas as she could, careful not to trip on
the cobblestones beneath her feet. She was breathing
hard and her heart was pounding as sweat streamed
down her back and strands of her hair stuck to her
forehead and cheeks. Henny was exhausted and
frightened when Lukas came to a stop in front a plain
gray door so suddenly that she nearly ran into him.
He paused, looked around, and then rapped on the
door in what seemed to be a coded knock: three short
taps, a pause, and then three more. A moment later,
the door opened and Lukas entered, pulling Henny
inside behind him.

She walked into a brightly lit room filled with
people. There were small groups of men and women
huddling here and there, seated on low chairs that
had been pulled together into tight circles. A tele-
phone rang incessantly in one corner of the room.
Maps were unfurled on several tables. A chalkboard
stood against one wall, filled with notes and arrows
and the names of several of the railway stations
in Copenhagen and other cities. Henny blinked,
adjusting to the bright light and the buzz of activity
and energy that bombarded her.

Lukas still hadn't said a word. He scanned the
room and then guided Henny over to two people

seated behind a small wooden desk at the far end. "Henny, this is Astrid and this is Vincent," he said, placing her in front of the desk. "They're the ones in charge of this operation. This is Henny Sinding. She's the one I told you about."

Astrid stood and reached out to shake Henny's hand. She was tall, with the brightest red hair Henny had ever seen. "Lukas told us all about you. You're impressive, especially with all of your sailing skills. Welcome. We're happy for any help we can get."

Henny returned the handshake, her head spinning with the knowledge that Astrid had questioned Lukas about her. She figured it was necessary to make sure she was someone to be trusted. Then, Henny turned to Vincent, who was also on his feet. He was just as tall as Astrid, with deep-set eyes that seemed to bore right through her.

"You do understand how dangerous this work is, don't you?" he asked. Henny squirmed under his piercing stare.

"Vincent, stop scaring Henny off before she's even done anything," said Astrid, leaning closer to Henny. "Don't be put off by my husband. He can be a little gruff. We're all here to help one another. And safety is our prime concern."

Henny liked her immediately.

"I thought Henny could come with me on the first

few missions," said Lukas. "I'll keep an eye on her and show her what we do."

"That's a good idea," Astrid replied, turning to Henny once more. "Lukas is one of our best soldiers. He'll show you the ropes. Now go meet everyone, Henny. You may find a few others that you already know."

Henny barely heard what Astrid said; her head was reeling at the words *soldier* and *mission*. What had she gotten herself into?

"Come on," Lukas said, taking Henny by the arm once more. "I'll introduce you around. And we'll get information on what we're meant to do tonight."

He led her across the room, introducing her to about a dozen young men and women, some her age, some older, each one shaking her hand and welcoming her as if she were joining a club. She didn't say much. In fact, she'd barely said a word since arriving. Everything felt overwhelming and unfamiliar, and scary. She still didn't know what this mission was that she was about to undertake with Lukas. And all her resolve about wanting to do something important to stand up to the Nazis was beginning to falter. At the same time, everyone seemed so confident and calm. She could do this; she kept telling herself. She had to do this. Daring and brave. She couldn't forget why she was here.

"And I think you know these two," Lukas finally said.

Henny turned and came face to face with the twins, Emma and Sophia. Her mouth dropped open. "Are you two part of this, as well?"

They smiled in unison. "It's about time you became part of our group," Emma said, pushing her glasses back up on her nose.

Sophia glanced across the room. "Those are our parents. We've been coming to these meetings for quite a while."

Henny followed her look and gasped. "Astrid and Vincent? Your parents?" She noted Astrid's red hair and the way she tilted her head when she was listening to someone—just like the twins.

They nodded. "Don't let our dad scare you. He's the more serious one in the family," Emma said. "But we're all doing really important work. We wondered when you'd join us."

There was no time for more conversation. Astrid and Vincent—the twins' parents—were calling the group to gather in front of the chalkboard.

"You've all had a chance to meet our new recruit, Henny," Astrid began when everyone had assembled and the last bit of chatter had died away. All eyes turned to Henny, who smiled nervously.

Astrid continued. "As you all know, we're here to speak out against the occupation of our country by the Nazis. And we're here to stand in solidarity against the oppression of our Jewish friends and neighbors. We don't have much time, and we need to get out onto the streets. I'll let Vincent describe the assignments for tonight. Then, you'll get into teams."

With that, she stepped aside, and Vincent moved in front of the group. "Tonight is a night to spread the word about who the Nazis really are."

He turned to the chalkboard and began to write down the names of several buildings in Copenhagen—businesses, banks, schools—some whose names Henny recognized and others that were unfamiliar to her.

When he was satisfied with his list, Vincent turned back to the group "These are the buildings we'll target tonight. Plaster the doors and windows with our literature. Leave piles of pamphlets in places where the citizens of Copenhagen will be able to read them in the morning. You'll team up in pairs."

Lukas smiled and winked at Henny while all around her, the young people began to pair off. The twins linked arms; they were not going to be separated. Once the groups were formed, they came forward and grabbed armfuls of pamphlets along with tins of paste. Lukas did the same, handing some pamphlets over to Henny. Then, the groups all headed to the door.

"Watch out for one another. And above all, be careful out there," Astrid called.

Henny followed Lukas out the door and down an alley. Her heart was still pounding, and uncertainty had wrapped its arms around her like a clamp, squeezing her chest so hard it was taking her breath away. She had to get a grip, try to calm down and focus on the task at hand.

Once again, Lukas wove his way through the backstreets of the city until they finally stood in front of an imposing brick building. Henny knew what it was: the post office, one of the main buildings in Copenhagen. During the day, it pulsed with Danish citizens going in and out, dropping letters and parcels, picking up mail, sending telegrams. It was one of the busiest buildings in the city.

Henny paused beside Lukas. "What do we do now?" she whispered.

Lukas looked around and Henny followed his glance. The streets were dark except for one lone street lamp across the way. Its light flickered on and off like a nervous twitch. No one was about.

"Let's start with the windows," Lukas finally said. "You hold the papers, and I'll stick them on."

The two of them moved to the row of windows stretching on either side of the post office door. Following Lukas's instructions, Henny held one sheet of paper up against the first window, and Lukas glued it on with a quick swipe of a brush from his can of paste. Only then did Henny stand back to read what was written.

People of Denmark!
Rise up against the Nazi invaders
before they take over our country.
Their ideals are evil.
Their leaders are criminals.
Stand together against them
and we will remain free and strong!

At the bottom of the pamphlet was a swastika that had been crossed out with thick, black strokes, just like the paper that Henny had seen in Lukas's bag, days earlier.

"Come on," Lukas whispered, more urgently this time. "We've got to move."

One after another, Henny held the paper up

against the windows, while Lukas glued them it place. Henny began to lose count of how many they were posting. A dozen? A hundred? Five hundred? But, with each paper, her resolve and excitement for the task grew and grew.

They must have worked for more than an hour. It was close to midnight by the time they finished. Thankfully, at this late hour, no one was around. But, every now and then, she glanced over her shoulder, wondering if a Nazi patrol would appear and arrest them. The dread that Henny had felt earlier that evening returned, hovering like a cloud over her head. She tried with all her might to push it away and tell herself that what she was doing was worth some level of fear. She and Lukas stood back from the building. Against the darkness, the white sheets of paper stood out, faintly glowing off the windows.

Far had once taken Henny to an exhibition of abstract art by the painter Wassily Kandinsky. His paintings were a series of cubes and lines that seemed, at first, strange to her. "It doesn't make sense," she had complained to Far. "Anyone can do that."

"Just look more closely," Far had instructed her. "It will start to make sense if you just stand and observe, and let the painting come to you."

That's what Henny had done, and before long,

the cubes began to resemble buildings, and the lines looked like streets, and the chaos of the painting began to seem right to her. The post office, with its black outline and white paper shapes, reminded her of that. It looked like art.

Lukas stood next to her, looking over at the building. "I'd say our work is done here," he said.

Henny's eyes shone as brightly as the white sheets of paper dotting the building. Her heart began to pound again. But this time, the feeling that she experienced was pure exhilaration. She was doing something! She wasn't keeping her head in the sand. She was standing up to the Nazis. Daring and brave. She felt both!

She stared at their handiwork and said, "I should have done this a lot sooner!"

CHAPTER 10

Over the next several weeks, Henny continued to accompany Lukas on his nighttime operations with the Resistance. Their routine was becoming second nature to her. Lukas would pass by her at school and mouth the word *tonight*. She'd meet up with him at exactly ten o'clock, and together they would make their way to the safe meeting place, receive their orders from Vincent and Astrid, then go out into the streets of Copenhagen to plaster key buildings with pamphlets. Lukas had said that he would work together with her for the first few outings, just so she could learn the ropes. But they had remained as a team. And Henny liked that. She felt safe with him, even though she wondered at times if this work was satisfying enough for Lukas. Others in the Resistance were breaking into Nazi buildings to steal guns and other weapons, or forging documents for those planning subversive actions, or any other number of perhaps more risky activities. Was Henny keeping Lukas from doing something more dangerous—more important—than papering buildings?

"Everything in the Resistance is important," Lukas assured her.

By the time their missions were done, it was usually past midnight. She often slept over at the twins' house, and they were only too happy to have her stay with them. Their house was usually dark and quiet when they arrived. Henny could never tell if Astrid and Vincent were already home and asleep, or if they were still out working. In the morning, the twins' parents would be in the kitchen preparing breakfast. Astrid would ask if Henny had slept well. Vincent would ask if anything special was happening at school that day. No one ever spoke about the previous night's activities.

Similarly, Henny never asked Emma and Sophia much about their parents or how they had become involved with the Resistance movement, though she often wondered if Astrid and Vincent worried about their children's safety. How could they not worry? But the twins never volunteered any information.

It was an unspoken agreement that no one ever talked about any other group member. Protecting one another's identity and safety was of utmost importance.

Mor and Far questioned Henny now and then about spending so much time at the twins' house. "So many nights," Mor said, one evening as Henny was about to head out the door.

"Trust me, Mor," Henny replied, trying to sound more sure than she felt. "It's important for me to do this."

"Perhaps they could sleep over here one night," Far suggested.

Henny shook her head. "It's just so much easier if I go there. Their house is much closer to school." That part, at least, was true.

"Well, I imagine your grades are going to be much better this term," Mor said.

"Your mother and I are so proud that you have become so serious about your schoolwork," Far added.

Henny looked away. She felt guilty keeping the truth from her parents. At the same time, she wondered if they suspected anything about what she was really doing. It was unlike them not to question her more thoroughly. And despite her promise to Lukas and her vow to the group, a part of Henny almost wished they would ask. It might have given her an excuse to confess everything to Mor and Far— to include them somehow. But they didn't ask, and Henny knew she couldn't tell them anything. She did worry about school. She knew she had better do well. Otherwise, what was all this extra "studying" for?

One night, Henny met up with Lukas as usual. They were scheduled to plaster a school with pamphlets warning that the Nazis would get rid of their beloved King Christian if the citizens of Denmark did not resist. Henny and Lukas covered every window of the school building with sheets of paper, and they did it in record time. They barely needed to say a word to one another. They communicated with a knowing look and a quick nod. They'd become almost as good at reading each other's minds as the twins were.

They finished their work and realized that they still had a bunch of pamphlets left over.

"I think we've covered every inch of this building," Henny said. She looked down at the papers in her hand. "What are we going to do with these?"

"I have an idea," Lukas replied.

Without saying a word, he guided Henny back to

the center of the city and onto one of the old stone bridges of Copenhagen. Henny and Lukas stopped in the middle of the bridge and looked over the stone railing. Below, the streets were quiet. There was no tension in the air, no hint that the Nazis could overwhelm this country with their military power. The only sound was the faint buzzing of insects around a nearby street lamp.

"What are we doing here?" Henny asked. There were no buildings on the bridge, nowhere to post their remaining pamphlets. There was only a road in the center for cars and two small paths for pedestrians on either side. The overpass allowed commuters to walk over the busy road below without having to compete with daytime traffic.

Lukas pointed at the papers that Henny still held in her hand. "Throw them over the edge," he said.

"What?"

"Toss them into the air. People will get a nice surprise when they walk to work in the morning and they pick up one of these, don't you think?" he asked. "We'll give them something interesting to read for their morning walk."

Henny hesitated, and then a slow smile spread across her face. With Lukas watching, she tossed the handful of remaining brochures high into the air and watched as they rained down onto the road, dividing up and scattering like springtime pollen in the light breeze. The sheets of paper remained suspended in the air, and then landed on the bridge around them, on the sidewalk and road below, and even on a few benches and chairs that had been left in front of several cafés.

Henny grinned, imagining men and women making their way to work the next morning, bending down to pick up a paper, and reading the text denouncing the Nazis. A feeling of delight filled her body, knowing that she was spreading the message of how evil they were, knowing that she was standing up for the freedom of Denmark. She felt bolder and more confident than she had ever felt before.

"It feels good, doesn't it?" Lukas asked. "Doing something for the cause?"

Closing her eyes, she let her head fall back and allowed the moment to wash over her.

In the silence that followed, they suddenly heard the faint purr of a motor approaching. She locked eyes with Lukas.

He glanced around. They were in the middle of the overpass in the middle of the night. The approaching car had to be the police or a Nazi patrol of some kind. No one else was out driving at this time. There was nowhere for Henny and Lukas to run and nothing to hide behind. If a car came up and saw them, they would be exposed. And if the papers they had thrown on the bridge and onto the street below were discovered and traced back to them, not only would they be in big trouble, but the whole Resistance movement might be jeopardized.

The sound of the motor was growing louder. They couldn't wait another second. Lukas grabbed Henny by the hand, and together they began to run across the overpass toward the road on the other side. The sound of the motor continued to build, like a deep growl rumbling louder by the second behind them. How close was the car? Henny couldn't look back. She knew she would stumble if she did. Her heart was pounding, her breath coming in quick, shallow pants. She clutched Lukas's hand, trying to keep up with his long stride.

She could see the end of the overpass. Would they have enough time to make it to the other side without being seen? Lukas was breathing hard next to her, his gasps competing with the sound of the motor still intensifying behind them. Ten steps away, then five, and finally, they reached the end of the path and dove behind a pillar just as the glare of headlights beamed across the darkened bridge.

Henny peered out from behind their hiding spot and saw that the car had paused in the middle of the bridge. She noted the swastika flags flying from the side windows. Nazi police! Had they seen the pamphlets still scattered around them? Had they seen her and Lukas throwing the papers wildly over the edge and then running for cover?

Henny buried her head in her arms, squeezing her body up against the stone column. She could feel Lukas next to her, pressing closer and encircling her with one arm.

Another second passed and the vehicle carried on, slower now as if the police inside were searching for someone—searching for her and Lukas! She heard the car tires crunching on the cobblestones as she pulled her head down and leaned even closer to Lukas. She couldn't breathe. Sweat rolled into her eyes. She thought she might throw up; she could feel the saliva thickening in her throat. Her arms and legs shook uncontrollably.

Approaching their hiding spot, the car slowed even more. Henny crouched lower, trying to make her body as small as possible. She squeezed her eyes shut; maybe if she didn't look, no one would see her, she thought wildly. Long terrible moments passed as she listened to the car idle next to her, until finally it revved its motor and sped on ahead.

Henny and Lukas still didn't move. Henny wasn't sure how many minutes passed before she finally raised her head. Lukas did the same. Then he stood, helping her to her feet next to him. She wasn't sure she would be able to stand; her legs still felt weak.

"That was too close for comfort," Lukas said.

Henny couldn't answer. She nodded, feeling her heart rate begin to return to normal and her breathing along with it.

"I don't think we should tell Astrid that we almost got caught," Lukas continued. "Perhaps we were a bit reckless to throw those pamphlets off the bridge."

"Thank goodness nothing happened," replied Henny.

The two of them turned and ran back to the meeting house. When Astrid asked about the evening, they said that everything had gone according to plan.

CHAPTER 11

Henny couldn't shake the feeling of having nearly been caught by the Nazis. For several nights after that, she lay half asleep, dreaming of patrol cars following her on the streets, chasing her down and throwing her into the back of their truck, shouting at her that she was a traitor and would be punished for her activities. She would bolt awake, sweating and trembling, clutching her blankets up to her face. Once, she cried out in her sleep. Mor came rushing in to her bedroom, shaking her awake from her nightmare.

"It must be all those late nights," Mor said after sitting with Henny until she had calmed down. "Perhaps you're studying too hard?" The worry lines around Mor's eyes seemed deeper than ever.

"I'm fine, Mor," Henny replied, trying her best to

sound cheerful. She hated to worry her mother like this. "Just a dream. I'll go back to sleep now."

Mor didn't seem convinced. But she nodded and left Henny's bedroom, leaving the door open a crack and switching on a hall light, just like she had done when Henny was a small child and didn't like to sleep in the dark.

Henny rolled over and closed her eyes. But she couldn't go back to sleep. The responsibility of every-thing she was doing weighed heavily on her. And the risks felt greater than ever. It's not that she wanted to stop; she didn't. Her resolve to stand up to the Nazis was still strong. But she had to find a way to deal with it all, to try to relax and not carry the images in her head like a bad movie that played over and over. She knew there was only one thing that would help. Sailing!

It had been weeks since Henny was able to join her father on his runs to the lighthouse. She had spent so many late nights working with the Resistance. And on those evenings when she wasn't on a mission, she felt too tired to do anything but eat, try to catch up on homework, and throw herself into bed. Far hadn't pushed her about coming with him. If he suspected she might be up to something else, he wasn't asking. So, a couple of days later at breakfast, she pushed her fatigue aside and said that she was going with him on a delivery to the lighthouse. Far didn't hide his pleasure.

"I think Gerda has missed you," he said. "I know Gerhardt and Otto have. And so have I, *min skat.*"

Far's eyes shone as he said this. For her reserved father, this was the closest to a hug that he could give.

"Otto and Gerhardt have missed teasing me," she replied, making light of the moment.

"I'm making a delivery this afternoon," Far continued. "Will you come?"

Henny nodded. "I'll meet you at the boat."

Far, Otto, and Gerhardt were already on board the *Gerda III* when Henny arrived at the pier that afternoon. She jumped on deck and, without asking, took her place behind the steering wheel. Otto and Gerhardt just grinned at her, released the lines that had secured Gerda to the dock, and leapt back on board. Far assumed his position at the bow of the boat, holding tightly to the mast with one hand and pointing in the direction for Henny to follow with the other.

Henny steered Gerda away from the pier and then revved the motor, taking the boat out into the channel. She pulled her jacket collar up against the wind. The weather in late September was still warm. But there were occasional days like this one, where the temperature would dip. Fall and winter were coming, Henny realized. Before long, these runs to the lighthouse would be less pleasant.

The traffic on the channel was busy as Henny steered the boat across. A sharp wind flung her hair wildly in all directions, and sprays of salt water misted her face. She breathed in the smell of fish mixed with seawater, as familiar to her as Mor's cooking. Slowly, she felt the tightness in her back and shoulders release as she veered upwind and downwind to avoid other boats that were motoring across. Oh, how she had missed this—missed the water and the chance to be on the channel, missed Gerda and the feel of the boat beneath her feet along with the steering wheel in her hands. This was just as important as resistance work was, she thought, too important to give up. Resistance work gave meaning to her life, but being on the water *was* her life!

All too quickly, they arrived at the lighthouse, and with the help of Otto and Gerhardt, Henny and her father began to unload the supplies from the hold. Several men from the lighthouse had come down to the pier today to help them. They grabbed boxes containing the food and other supplies. Far escorted the men up the path to the main building, leaving Henny on the dock with Otto and Gerhardt. They helped her back on board and followed her into the cabin.

"I was wondering when you were going to bring your neighbor Susanne out for a sail again," Otto asked. "I never thought I'd meet anyone who loved the sea as much as you do. But that little girl reminded me of you when you were younger."

"A mini version," Gerhardt added.

"I don't know," Henny replied. "I'd love to but ..."

"I hope she wasn't too scared seeing that Nazi boat on the water," said Otto.

Henny didn't really want to talk about the Nazis on a day when she was just there to enjoy the sea. But something was troubling her. "Otto, did you ever find out what happened to your friend? The one who was arrested?"

He shook his head. "No. But another neighbor of mine was also taken—a Jewish fellow. And I know he wasn't doing anything wrong. They arrested him just because he's Jewish." He scratched at his chin. "If we're not careful, Denmark will become another Poland and they'll start arresting Jews all over the place. It's a disgrace."

"I've said it before, and I'll say it again," added Gerhardt. "I'd do anything to find a way to stop the Nazis."

"Anything!" echoed Otto. He sighed heavily and then looked over at Henny. "It's so good to see you again. I guess you've been too busy lately to pay any attention to us," he joked.

"Maybe she's got a young man in her life," added Gerhardt.

"I thought I was the only man she had eyes for," Otto replied.

"You?" exclaimed Gerhardt. "You're too old and ugly for anyone to care about!"

Henny rolled her eyes. "You two are impossible. No, there is no 'young man' in my life." That wasn't entirely true, though. She was spending so much time with Lukas during their evening resistance raids. And now, he was even trying to help her with her school-work, not wanting her to fall too far behind. When they talked, she knew that they had the same goals in mind, the same idea about what their country should look like and who they should stand up to defend. She had never thought about him in any way other than as a friend. But perhaps that was changing. She turned back to Otto and Gerhardt. "And no, I'm not interested in either of you!"

Otto clutched at his heart in mock despair. "I'm wounded and devastated! I'll never recover."

All three of them laughed. She missed her time with these men as much as she missed sailing Gerda.

"Seriously, though," Otto continued. "Where have you been? It's not like you to give up these runs on the channel."

Henny's stomach tightened. She longed to tell the two of them what she was doing. Otto and Gerhardt were her friends—no, they were like brothers. But, she had vowed to tell no one. She hadn't even told Mor and Far, even though the secret weighed so heavily on her and the deception about where she went at night was getting harder to carry.

Henny sighed. "Just trying to catch up on some schoolwork. That's all." Henny caught a puzzled look that passed from Otto to Gerhardt, as if they knew that wasn't entirely true. She looked away. She couldn't tell them what she had been doing. She couldn't tell anyone. At least, not yet.

CHAPTER 12

Far was completely animated that night at dinner. He talked about the weather cooling down. He talked about the increased traffic on the channel, and he talked about the lighthouse. He was so happy that he didn't turn on the radio—something he had taken to doing most evenings—sparing them whatever news might spoil the good mood.

"Now, more than ever, we need to keep the lighthouse in the best working condition. The safety of those sailors on the water depends on it."

Far even had another joke for her. "What did the fish say when it swam into a wall?" he asked, his face lit up in a way that Henny rarely saw.

"Dam!" he blurted, without giving her a chance to respond.

"Such a terrible word," said Mor.

"No, no," Far replied. "Don't you get it? The fish thought it was swimming into a beaver dam. That's the joke."

"I get it, Far," Henny replied.

"Oh, Paul," Mor said. "It's so silly."

"But it's funny, right?"

"Yes, very funny," Henny said, not wanting to disappoint her father.

Mor had cooked all of Henny's favorites that evening. "It's a celebration because we are all home together!"

There were panfried sausages with boiled potatoes and red cabbage. Mor piled spoonful after spoonful on Henny's plate, urging her to eat until she thought she might explode. She wanted to please her mother. And the truth was, the food was delicious! There were some nights when she left home so early to meet with Lukas and the others that she had to skip her family dinner, lying to her parents yet again and telling them she would eat at the twins' house. The truth was that on those nights, she was lucky if they got a stale sandwich to hold them over. Not that she ever complained. But this feast was a treat.

The three of them were just finishing the creamy

rice pudding that Mor had made for dessert and were sipping some scalding-hot licorice tea when there was a sudden and urgent knock at the door.

Henny froze, her spoon midway to her mouth. She stared at Mor and Far, eyes widening. It was late—after nine o'clock. No one ever came to their door at this hour.

"I'll get it," Henny said, lowering her spoon and beginning to get up.

"No." Far reached out a hand to stop her. "Finish your dessert," he said, rising from the table. Mor followed, and after a moment, Henny did as well, anxious to see who was continuing to knock with such insistence. Far paused at the door, quickly straightened his tie, and opened it. Mr. Rubin stood on the other side.

He shifted his weight from one foot to the other, glancing down the street in both directions. "May I come in?" he asked. His voice was low and hoarse.

Far didn't hesitate. "Of course."

Mr. Rubin entered the hallway, removed his hat, and bowed to Mor. "I'm sorry to bother you so late at night." His brow was creased and his eyes shifted back and forth from Mor to Far.

"You're welcome here any time," Mor replied. "We were just having tea and dessert. Come and join us."

"You're very kind," Mr. Rubin said. "But, no. I need to get back to my family."

"What is it, Victor?" Far asked. "Is everything all right?"

Mr. Rubin lowered his eyes. When he looked up, Henny could see tears gathering in the corners. It scared her to see their neighbor on the verge of crying.

"No," Mr. Rubin replied. "I'm afraid everything is far from all right."

"Is someone sick?" Mor asked. "One of the children?"

"No, it's not our health." Mr. Rubin hesitated, seeming unsure of how to begin. Henny felt the muscles in her neck and back begin to constrict. The news, whatever it was, couldn't be good.

Mr. Rubin took a deep breath. "It's all over the radio. The Nazis have stepped in to dissolve our government. Denmark has declared a state of emergency."

"I didn't have the radio on this evening," Far replied, looking uneasy.

"There's more," Mr. Rubin said, shifting again from one foot to the other. "The Nazis have decided that it's time to get rid of all the Jews in Denmark."

Far's eyes widened. "But we've been hearing those

rumors for the last three years."

"Almost every week," Mor added.

Mr. Rubin shook his head. "This time, I'm afraid it's for real. Our rabbi spoke to us today in the synagogue. He has learned that the Nazis are going to start arresting Jewish families from their homes, and take men, women, and children off the streets."

There it was! All of the things that everyone had feared. First, the Nazis were assuming complete control of her country, and then, Jewish citizens would be targeted. Henny could have cried. All of her efforts with the Resistance, all of their messages to rise up against the evil Nazis, had accomplished nothing. She had been fooling herself to think it could. The truth was here in Mr. Rubin's terrifying disclosure. Her country was powerless against Hitler's rule. And he and his followers were about to prove that. In that moment, all the good feeling that Henny had from being on the water earlier that day flooded out of her in one whoosh.

"They're planning raids," Mr. Rubin continued. "Sometime in the near future. No one will be safe." Mr. Rubin hung his head once more. "You know about the concentration camps in Poland and Germany—those terrible prisons where Jews are being killed. They're calling them death camps.

Do you think it's true?" he asked, looking at them now, his eyes full of fear.

No one answered.

"If we're arrested, I imagine we'll all be taken there, men, women, and even the children." He whispered the last word.

A shudder rippled through Henny's body. She had a fleeting image of Susanne—sweet, young Susanne, along with Aron. It was hard enough to think about adults like Mr. Rubin being arrested and sent away to some terrible fate. But what would the Nazis do if they got their hands on the children?

"The disbanding of the government is public information," Mr. Rubin added. "But the arrest of the Jewish citizens hasn't been made public. The Nazis are trying to keep that a secret so that they can raid our homes without our knowing that they're coming. Our rabbi found out only because someone on the inside told him."

"Thank goodness for that, at least," Mor exclaimed. "We can try to prepare."

"It doesn't change what's going to happen," said Mr. Rubin, shaking his head. "With our government no longer in power, there is no one to protect us. No one to protect my family ..." His voice trailed off.

"But we can try to organize something, now that

we know about this," Far added. "What can we do to help?"

Mr. Rubin shook his head. "There are many in my community who are trying to figure out how we can leave the city—perhaps try to find a place to stay where we can be safe."

"You're going to leave Copenhagen?" Henny croaked out the question.

"What choice do we have?"

"But where will you go?"

"Some are already running to the woods to hide. They say that Sweden may be a safe place to go. The Nazis haven't taken it over—at least, not yet."

Sweden! The country across the channel. Would it really provide a safe haven to thousands of Danish Jews? And how could everyone get there? And if they could figure out a way to do it, would there even be enough time to escape? The questions galloped through Henny's mind as she stood staring at Mr. Rubin.

Far was speaking. "We'll help in any way we can."

Mr. Rubin nodded. "We still need to get organized, talk, plan. We don't know how much time we have." He reached out to grab Far's hand as tears gathered once more in his eyes. "I'm afraid we're living on borrowed time. I wanted you to know all of this. You've always been a friend, and so kind to us. I may come to you, asking for that kindness again."

"We're here for you," Far replied as he escorted Mr. Rubin to the door.

Before leaving, Mr. Rubin turned to face Henny and her parents once more. "The Nazis have done whatever they want with Jews in every other country around Europe. How could we have thought it would be any different here?"

With that, he put his hat back on, bowed once more, and left. Far turned, took Mor by the arm, and walked back into the dining room. Henny could hear the radio spring to life as Far began to search for the news station.

Henny rushed out the door, calling out to Mr. Rubin, who was walking away from her house at a quick pace. She caught up with him and paused.

"Please tell Susanne I'm thinking of her. I still want to take her sailing again. It's something I promised."

Mr. Rubin smiled sadly. "I pray that day will come."

CHAPTER 13

When Henny returned home and joined her parents seated in the dining room, a radio announcer was reviewing the details of Denmark's complete surrender to the Nazis. Just as Mr. Rubin had said, the military was now in power. The administration of Denmark was in the hands of Nazi Germany.

Mor's face was filled with pain. The worry lines around her eyes and mouth seemed to have deepened in the last few minutes. Far looked equally distraught.

"That's it, then," he said, leaning forward to switch off the radio. A tense silence filled the dining room. "Our country is no more. The Nazis have won."

"I can't believe this is happening here," Mor said, lowering her head into her hands.

Far reached out to touch her arm. It was a physical

gesture that Henny rarely saw. "I truly believed that Denmark would stay safe. But Hitler is a madman, unpredictable and hungry for power."

"And the Jewish families?" asked Mor, looking up.

Far shook his head. "I don't know what we're going to be able to do to help them."

Henny's mind was racing a mile a minute. Her neighbors were in danger, as well as Jewish families Henny didn't even know. Whether she knew them or not, they were all fellow citizens. And now, they needed protection.

"But there must be something, Paul," Mor pleaded. "Is there anyone you can talk to? Perhaps someone in the navy?"

Far shook his head. "If the Nazis come for the Jews, I don't think anyone in the navy or any other division will be able to help them. All we can do is pray that they will stay safe. Perhaps leaving for Sweden, as Susanne's father said they would try to do, is the only solution. But I don't even know how they'd get there."

Henny, silent up until now, stared at her father. "Sweden?"

He nodded. "Yes. It's a neutral country."

"And if Jewish families could find a way to get there, they'd be safe?"

Far nodded again.

Henny had an idea, something she knew she could do to help. It would require her friends in the resistance movement. But, more than that, it would require her father's involvement too. And that just wasn't possible. To tell her parents about her resistance work would mean breaking the promise—the oath—that she had taken to keep the secret of their work safe. And to involve her parents would jeopardize their safety too.

But what good was secrecy if her neighbors were in danger of being arrested? And wasn't the purpose of the Resistance to help those in need? During her very first meeting, Vincent and Astrid had said that they were there to stand in solidarity against the oppression of their Jewish friends and neighbors. Henny took that vow as seriously as she took the oath of silence. Now was the time to demonstrate just how important the Resistance could be.

The details of her idea were fuzzy and still unclear. And she knew that she should probably take all of this to Vincent and Astrid first—sort it out with her resistance partners. But, in order for her plan to work at all, she would need her parents' help. She had to speak up now.

Taking a deep breath, she began. "Mor, Far, there's something I have to tell you."

"We know you're worried about Susanne," Far said. "We're worried too, but—"

"No," Henny interrupted. "I mean, yes, of course I'm worried. But that's not what I want to say. I need you to listen to me and not say a word until I'm finished talking." She turned her face away from the looks in her parents' eyes—fear bordering on panic.

And then she told them—about seeing the sheets of paper inside Lukas's book bag that day so many weeks earlier and how she had questioned him about it. She told them how he had talked of his involvement with the resistance group, and how she had begged him to take her along after seeing the Jewish man taken from the street. She talked about Astrid and Vincent and the safe meeting place where they received their instructions. She talked about all the activities that the group was involved in. And she talked about her own job distributing anti-Nazi pamphlets across the city, papering the windows and doors of building after building, with Lukas by her side. She confessed it all, and then stopped and waited for her parents to speak.

"I can't believe the danger you've been putting yourself in," Mor finally said after Henny's confession had sunk in. "You could have been caught! And then, who knows what might have happened to you."

"I know it's dangerous, Mor. But I've been doing this for our country. And for those in our country who are losing their power and their rights. Isn't it worth taking a risk for those people?"

She turned to her father, who was still quiet. "Far, you once said that you respected each and every person who stood up to the Nazis—that those resisters might be the ones to save our country. That's what I've been trying to do."

Far's eyes were still troubled. "So, all those nights you said you were studying at Emma and Sophia's house? That was a lie?"

Henny nodded. "I knew you wouldn't let me go. So I had to make up some kind of excuse for being out. The twins are part of the group as well. Their parents got them involved a long time ago," she added weakly, hoping that might make it better.

Silence filled the room once more. Mor and Far stared at one another, seeming to pass an unspoken message back and forth. Henny waited, watching them. She was glad she had told her parents everything; it was a relief to get it off her chest, to stop the deception. But what now? After what felt like forever, Far finally sighed deeply and turned to Henny.

"I'm glad you've told us this. We would rather know than not know."

And then he said something that made Henny's heart swell.

"I have to tell you that your mother and I are very proud of you. Scared about what might happen," he added, "but still, ever so proud." His voice caught and faltered.

"But why are you telling us this now?" Mor asked.

Henny braced herself. "I have an idea—something that I can do to help the Rubins and others."

Far looked puzzled. "What can you possibly do?"

Henny swallowed hard. "You talked about Sweden and so did Mr. Rubin—a place where it may be safer for Jewish families."

Far nodded. "Hopefully, Sweden will remain neutral."

"I know a way that the Rubins can get there," Henny declared.

A fly buzzed close to a lamp in the dining room. It must have flown in the door with Mr. Rubin, Henny thought. The fly hit the bulb, recoiled, and then hit it again, back and forth, popping against the light bulb until it finally fell to the tabletop, landing on its back. There, it buzzed around in a circle until it fell silent.

"The *Gerda III*," Henny continued. "It can take a group of people to safety, sailing them across the channel to Sweden. They can hide in the hold below deck. No one will see them." It was a perfect plan, she reasoned. The Rubin family needed a way to get to Sweden and Gerda could provide the perfect vessel to take them out of Copenhagen.

The silence that followed this declaration was even more overwhelming than before. Mor was the first to speak.

"That's impossible! Henny, you could all be arrested!"

"We can't possibly do this," Far added.

"Besides," Mor continued, "if the boat was boarded by the Nazis, your father's position would be jeopardized. He could be arrested as well."

"Your mother's right," Far said. "It's not that I don't want to help. I do! But this may be too much."

"I know you want to do something, but this is simply too dangerous," Mor said, her voice dropping to a whisper.

Or course, it was dangerous, Henny thought. Any mission against the Nazis was dangerous. But that wasn't the point. The point was trying to do anything in her power to help—even if it meant that there were risks involved. There was so much to think about. And so much to plan. She could rescue other Jewish families, too, with Mr. Rubin's help. Hopefully, Astrid and Vincent would be able to coordinate with a group in Sweden to help the Jews once they got across the channel. She knew they had contacts in other countries.

But Henny was getting ahead of herself. First, she needed to talk to her group, and talk to Lukas. And that meant she would have to tell them she had confessed their activities to her parents. Would they understand? They had to! Henny glanced at the small table lamp. The fly had disappeared; maybe it had gotten its second wind and taken off to freedom. The notion, silly as it was, gave her hope. She turned to her father.

"Far, do you believe that what I'm wanting to do is important?"

Far hesitated. "Yes, of course, but ..."

"And do you believe that my group wouldn't plan anything unless we had considered every possible danger?"

Far hesitated again, and then slowly nodded.

"Then, please trust me," Henny said.

Far glanced at his wife, and then hung his head. "We do," he said weakly.

"I know it's a lot to think about," Henny said, reaching out to grab her parents' hands. "Your trust means so much to me. Once I've had a chance to gather more information, we'll talk again."

CHAPTER 14

Henny went looking for Lukas at school first thing the next morning. He was standing with the twins, leaning against the school building as they usually did in the morning. She could tell by the looks on their faces that they, too, had heard the news of the government overthrow. Here and there around the schoolyard, groups of students were clustered together, some holding newspapers with headlines that announced the Nazi military had seized control of the government. Henny imagined that everyone in the country knew by now. But hardly anyone knew of the Nazi plan to arrest all Jewish citizens. She whispered this information to Lukas and the twins as she joined them in their huddle. To her surprise, they already knew about it.

"How did you hear?" Henny asked, keeping her voice low.

"I went to the resistance house last night and Astrid told me," Lukas replied. "She has contacts that none of us know about. How did you find out?"

Henny explained how her Jewish neighbor had come over the night before bearing the terrible news.

"The Nazis are monsters," Emma declared, adjusting her glasses. "They don't care about anyone except themselves."

"And getting as much power as they can," Sophia added.

"No matter who stands in their way!" The twins recited this last statement in unison.

"Our resistance is even more important now," Lukas said, pushing his hair off his face. "We have to find more ways to fight for our people, and to fight for our Jewish friends and neighbors."

This was the opportunity Henny was looking for, a chance to tell her friends about her plan to bring Jewish families to safety in Sweden aboard the *Gerda III*. But to do that, she would first have to tell them that she had told her parents about her activities with the Resistance—implicating them all in the plan. She still didn't know if they would stand with her on this decision. She didn't know if they would be angry with her and want her out of their group. What she *did* know was that with or without their help, she was determined to rescue the Rubin family—and others, if possible. She wanted to have the Resistance behind her.

Perhaps she should wait to talk to Astrid and Vincent first about all of this. But she was simply bursting with her idea and needed to get it out. Maybe, testing the information out on her friends before taking it to Astrid and Vincent was the better thing to do. At least, she hoped so.

"You're right," she began. "We have to help the Jewish citizens of our country. And I know a way that we can."

"Tell us," the twins cried.

Henny told them about the *Gerda III* and her idea to sail it to Sweden, carrying some Jewish families on board. As she spoke, she could see how supportive her friends were of her plan. Maybe she could delay talking about having revealed the Resistance to her parents.

Lukas's face lit up with excitement. "Have you ever sailed to Sweden before?"

"Only once. It's not an easy trip. The channel is choppy, and lately, there have been so many more Nazi boats out there."

Lukas nodded. "It sounds like it could be dangerous."

"Isn't everything we do dangerous?" Henny asked.

No one replied.

"This could save lives," Henny continued.

That's when Emma spoke up. "How will you ever sneak the boat away without letting your father know?" she asked.

Henny took a deep breath and faced her friends. After a tense pause, she said it. "I told my parents."

"Told them what?" the twins asked.

"I told them everything—the Resistance, Lukas, the two of you, Astrid, Vincent," she began. "I know how important our pact it," she rushed to add as the twins' faces went pale and Lukas froze. "But, if this plan is going to work, I need my parents—especially my father—to be on our side. And I know that he is."

The twins lowered their heads and looked away. Only Lukas stared at her, his gaze sweeping across her face and then coming to rest squarely in her eyes. He was breathing heavily, in and out, his nostrils flaring slightly. A cold prickle of fear traveled up Henny's spine. Was Lukas turning against her? That would be devastating. He was her friend and her partner in the Resistance. He had to understand—they all did—how important this admission was. They had to believe that telling her parents was going to help them in the long run.

It felt as if an eternity of time passed. And then Lukas nodded and said, "It was the right thing to do."

Henny exhaled the breath she had been holding.

"And it's a good plan," the twins declared. Henny could have hugged them.

"Crazy, for sure," Lukas added. "But good. We'll have to talk about it tonight."

"Of course!" Henny cried. Inside, she prayed that Astrid and Vincent would be as understanding and supportive as Lukas and the twins were. She turned to Emma and Sophia. "Please don't say anything to your parents. I have to be the one to tell them everything." They nodded.

Lukas smiled. "I knew your sailing would come in handy for us. I just wasn't sure how. Now I know."

"I guess there's no point in telling your parents that you're coming over to our house to study," Emma added.

Henny smiled, her first smile since they had gathered to talk. In fact, it was the first time she had smiled since yesterday, when she'd taken Gerda out for a run with her father to the lighthouse, before all the bad news, before everything in her country had changed for the worse.

The school bell rang, and Emma and Sophia raced ahead. As Henny and Lukas walked toward the school door, Erik came up beside them.

"You seemed to be having some kind of important meeting out there," he said.

Henny frowned and then turned toward him so that she could look him in the eyes.

"Just talking. You're always welcome to join us."

Erik smiled, shrugged his shoulders, and then said, "I know you're friends with that Jewish girl in the elementary school."

The comment came out of nowhere. It was the same thing that Lukas had once said to Henny. But, spoken by Erik, it felt more like a threat.

"What's wrong with that?" Henny asked. Her skin suddenly prickled with anger.

Erik shrugged. "My father says that Jews will take over the world if we let them. And we can't!"

"Erik, what are you taking about," Henny cried. "Susanne is ten years old! She's no threat."

"She could grow up to become one."

"How can you say something like that?"

Henny could see that Lukas was fuming. He glanced at her, and then turned and pushed his way through the doors of the school. She figured he must have thought it was better to walk away than confront

Erik and say something he might regret.

As for Henny, she was furious as well. Erik, always the quiet one, had suddenly found his voice. And what he was saying was terribly upsetting. She struggled to keep her voice even as she responded. "It seems to me that the Nazis are the ones taking over the world, not the Jews."

Erik shrugged again. Finally, he turned his back to her and walked inside.

CHAPTER 15

Henny had no time to think about Erik or his remarks about Jews. It had to have been ignorance that prompted the comment, she reasoned. More importantly, she was meeting with her group that evening, and she was still nervous about telling Astrid and Vincent that she had talked to her parents about her activities with the Resistance.

She needn't have worried about Astrid. She barely blinked when Henny, with Lukas by her side, confessed that she had told her parents about wanting to use the *Gerda III* to take some Jewish families to Sweden. In fact, Astrid agreed that it was a good plan. Vincent, however, wasn't so supportive.

"You actually told your parents about our activities? What happened to your vow to tell no one?" he asked heatedly.

Henny's face reddened and a flash of anger surged through her. "I've done everything for this cause, including lying to my parents about being here. And I've done it because I believe in what I'm doing. I've never questioned you or anyone."

Astrid jumped in to face Vincent. "If this is going to work, then we need Henny's parents to be on board. And we have to trust that she knows what she's doing."

Henny glared at Vincent, refusing to back down. She could be just as strong and stubborn as he was. Finally, he lowered his head and ran a hand through his hair.

"Sorry. I guess I'm just on edge with all the news of the Nazi roundup." He looked up. "Yes, I understand why you felt you had to tell them." He held his hand out to Henny. "Truce?" She nodded and accepted the handshake.

The group talked into the night, not only about Henny's plan with the *Gerda III*, but about other ways that they might be able to help the Jews of Denmark: smuggling them to safe houses in and around the city, moving them from place to place, finding other good citizens of Copenhagen who would help. At the same time, they vowed to continue to send out pamphlets denouncing the efforts of the Nazis and urging the citizens of Copenhagen to resist.

By the time the meeting ended, there were several proposals in place.

As to Henny's plan, the Jews would need help once they arrived in Sweden. "We're going to have to connect with our friends and colleagues over there, let them know we're developing a plan to sail Jewish refugees across the channel. We have groups in Sweden who will need to prepare to receive the families," Vincent said as the evening was wrapping up. It was just what Henny had hoped he would say.

"The one thing we don't know is when the round-up is going to happen," Astrid added, before sending everyone off. "We have to assume it will be soon. So, time is of the essence. Stay alert, everyone. And stay safe."

It was nearly midnight when Henny finally made her way back home. Her parents knew where she had been this time, so there was really no need to sneak in. Still, she opened the door as softly as she could, creeping through the hallway and into the kitchen. Not surprisingly, her parents were waiting for her when she entered.

Mor's face looked as drawn and anxious as it had the day before. Far paced back and forth, his face as strained as Mor's, though he was doing his best to hide it. Henny felt for them both. They were already worried enough about what was happening to their country. It couldn't have been easy for them to hear that their daughter was involved in high-risk activities with the Resistance. She wished she could take the pain away from them and ease their troubled minds. But sadly, she feared things were only going to get more difficult.

"So? What did your ... your group say?" Far asked after Mor had put tea out on the table and urged Henny to sit and drink.

She took a gulp. The hot liquid scalded her tongue. She blew on the drink before answering. "They think it's a good idea to rescue Jewish families with the *Gerda III*. And they're willing to help."

A bead of sweat dotted Far's forehead. "I'm glad they want to help. And I'm proud of all your efforts." He closed his eyes. "But, I'm still scared for you."

"I know you are," said Henny. "I wish there was some way to reassure you—and me too. But, there isn't." She shifted uneasily. "And there's something else. They want me to do a test run of the *Gerda III*," she said cautiously. "Take her across the channel without any passengers on board and see what the traffic is like out there, how many boats are sailing and what kinds ..." Her voice trailed off.

"They mean, how many Nazi boats are out there," Far finished her sentence.

Henny nodded. "It'll give us a better idea of how safe this will be."

It had been Astrid's idea to do the test run, and it was a good one, though it frightened Henny more than she was willing to say. She needed to take the boat out late at night—something she wasn't used to doing. She had no idea how busy the channel was at night, or if Nazi patrols were out at that time. Plus, she needed to test the boat on the choppy ride to Sweden and see if she could navigate through the difficult waters over to the other side. A test run across the channel would give her so much information about which route to take, when to go, and how to maneuver Gerda. And it would tell her if she really was capable of doing this.

Far's face looked grimmer than ever. "Yes, I understand. I'll have to figure out when I can take the Gerda out at night and—"

"No, Far," Henny interrupted. "You don't understand. You can't come with me. We don't want you mixed up in this plan any more than you have to be. It could threaten your position with the navy. Mor said it herself. I don't want you to put yourself in that position."

"But how can you do this without me?" Far asked. "You've only sailed across to Sweden once. And do you remember how hard it was? You had to hand the boat over to me."

"I'm going to talk to Otto and Gerhardt," Henny said. "Ask them to join me."

She knew that they hated the Nazis as much as she did. They had even talked about wanting to do something to fight back. And she trusted them like family. Besides, they could sail Gerda as well as or better than she could. If anyone could help her navigate across the channel, they were ones to do the job. She had told Astrid and Vincent about this idea. Vincent had grumbled at first about including anyone else in the plan. "Why don't we just advertise what we're doing in every newspaper in the city?" he had asked. But in the end, he too had accepted the idea.

"But surely, if anything happens, their jobs will be at risk as well," Far said.

Henny nodded. "Yes, though I think the Nazis would be more interested in you, given your position as an officer in the navy. It will be their choice, of course. But, I have a feeling Otto and Gerhardt are going to want to do this, no matter what the risk. Besides, you're the one who has always wanted them to come along with me when

I'm sailing Gerda," Henny pleaded with her father. "They're the perfect ones to join me now, if they're willing. And this way, we can keep you out of it as much as possible."

"I think it's a good idea." It was the first thing Mor had said since Henny came home.

Far looked at Henny, then back at Mor. He closed his eyes, squeezing them tightly together. Finally, he opened them and nodded.

Henny smiled gratefully. "All I need you to do is leave an extra key to the Gerda down at the pier. That way, I don't have to tell you when I'm taking her out."

CHAPTER 16

Almost overnight, it felt as if everything had changed in Copenhagen. The city was swarming with Nazi soldiers. They were everywhere—on Henny's walk to school and in front of every shop and bank and government building. They patrolled day and night. Astrid and Vincent had canceled all resistance activities; the risk of being caught was too high. The news reports were saying that King Christian was still on the throne. But he hadn't been seen for days. His rides through the city streets, waving at his subjects, had always been a source of comfort. His absence was another reminder that the Nazis were now fully in charge.

Henny decided that it was time to talk to Mr. and Mrs. Rubin. The Resistance was laying plans, as quickly as possible, to take them and other Jewish families to Sweden. One evening, as she prepared to go over to the Rubins' home, Far stopped her.

"Do you think it's a good idea to tell Mr. Rubin anything yet, when nothing is certain?" he asked.

"I just want to prepare him," she told her father. "But also, to make sure that he's not planning something else that could be riskier for his family."

She left her house, walked across the lawn, and knocked on the Rubins' door. No one answered. Henny knew they were home; she had seen Mr. Rubin enter the house several hours earlier. She waited a moment, then knocked again, louder and more insistent this time. On the other side, she heard footsteps approaching, and then nothing.

"It's Henny," she whispered from outside. "Please open the door."

Mrs. Rubin opened the door a crack and peered hesitantly from behind. She looked relieved when she saw who it was.

"My husband is lying down," she said, ushering Henny into the living room. "He doesn't want me to answer the door these days. He says you never know who might be on the other side." She looked down. "Perhaps it's foolish of us to be so cautious."

"Your husband is right to be careful," Henny said.

"Yes, well, I'm glad it's you," Mrs. Rubin replied. "Shall I make some tea?"

Henny shook her head. "This isn't a social call, Mrs. Rubin. But I would like your husband to be here when we talk."

Mrs. Rubin nodded and walked out of the room, leaving Henny alone. She wandered over to the piano, which sat in one corner. On it, there were framed photographs of the Rubin family: Mr. and Mrs. Rubin when they were first married, then Susanne as a baby, and more photos of her taken over the years. Henny paused in front of one. Susanne was sitting on a swing. Her head was back and her mouth was open as if she were laughing out loud. Her eyes were bright and as bold as ever. In later photos, she was joined by Aron, holding him in her arms as if he were hers, the same wide smile on both of their faces.

It was so unfair that children—Susanne and Aron—could be the target of the Nazis' hatred, Henny thought again as she stared at the collection of pictures. For Hitler and his followers to go after Jewish adults was terrible enough. But children? It made no sense.

There was a sudden movement behind her, and Henny turned to see Mr. Rubin enter the living room with his wife by his side. Henny gasped. Mr. Rubin seemed to have aged just in the last couple of days. The circles under his eyes were dark and deep, and his cheeks were pinched and sagging.

"I haven't had much sleep lately," he confessed.

Henny nodded sympathetically as he indicated the couch for her to sit. He and his wife perched on chairs opposite her.

"It's not as if I've been doing much work lately at my office. My clients—at least my Jewish clients—are reluctant to come out of their homes to meet with me. And who can blame them?"

"There are Nazi soldiers everywhere we look," his wife added. A veil of fear passed over her face.

Henny nodded again.

"We've been trying to organize our community," Mr. Rubin continued. "Figure out what we're going to do. We don't even know when anything is going to happen to us. But some members of our synagogue have already left, going into the countryside where they hope they will be safer. I'm not sure that will save them. According to our rabbi, the Nazis are vowing to arrest every Jewish person in the country."

"We can't pick up and run away like that," Mrs. Rubin said. "Our children are so young. We know we have to do something. But we're not sure what the best move for us is ..." Her voice trailed off.

"That's why I'm here," Henny said.

She didn't waste time. She told them about her involvement with the Danish Resistance. She didn't name names—only explained that a group was trying to organize to help save the Jews of the city. She told them she wanted to take them to Sweden by boat and that she was planning a test run in the next few days.

"You're right when you said that no one knows yet when the roundup of Jews will take place," Henny said. "I want you to know all of this so you'll be prepared to come with me on a moment's notice."

"On your boat?" Mrs. Rubin clasped her hands into a tight fist in her lap. "What about the children?"

"Of course, I'm talking about all of you, Susanne and Aron as well. And there may even be a couple of other families who come with us."

Mr. Rubin had grown silent. Finally, he leaned forward, his brow creased. "I have to ask, Henny, why are you the one to take us? Why not your father? It's not that we don't trust you," he hurried to add. "But he has so much more experience. And you're so young ..."

"My father knows what I'm planning to do, and he's very supportive." Henny didn't want to tell Mr. Rubin that it would put her father in too much danger if he were involved. "We've agreed that I can do this," she said. "I *want* to be the one to do this."

Another moment of silence passed. "And you think this is safe?" Mr. Rubin asked.

"You yourself talked about finding a way to get to Sweden. This is probably one of the only ways to get there," Henny replied. She didn't tell him about the difficult journey across the channel, or about the risk of running into a Nazi patrol on the water.

"I'm not sure about this, Victor," Mrs. Rubin said, her eyes searching her husband's face.

He looked grim. He stared back at his wife. Henny waited, wondering, hoping they would agree to her rescue plan. Finally, Mrs. Rubin sat back in her chair. Mr. Rubin turned to Henny.

"You have no idea how grateful we are that you're thinking of us like this, that you want to help save us." His voice shook and was gravelly with emotion. "Prepare as quickly as you can, Henny. We'll be ready for you."

Henny was just about to slip out the door of the Rubins' home when she was stopped by a tug on her arm. It was Susanne.

"Why are you still up?" Henny asked, glancing back at the living room where she had left Susanne's parents. They had moved over to sit on the couch. She could see Mr. Rubin, his arm wrapped tightly around his wife's shoulder. Both of them had their heads down and were completely still.

"I told you I can stay up as late as I want," Susanne replied. "It's only Aron who needs to go to bed early. And he's fast asleep. He's the baby, not me."

Henny smiled. "I know. You are almost grown-up."

Susanne nodded. "You're taking all of us away from here, aren't you? We're going to sail with you on Gerda."

Henny was taken aback. She glanced again at the living room. "You may be able to stay up late, Susanne, but I'm not sure you're supposed to be eavesdropping on your parents' conversations."

"I know what's been happening," Susanne said solemnly, her eyes round as two moons. "Mama and Papa think I don't know much, but I do."

Henny bit her lip tightly to stop the tears that she felt gathering behind her eyes. How was it possible to imagine Susanne's fate if she were to be arrested, rounded up, and sent to a concentration camp? "You have to try not to worry about any of this," she said, reaching out to take Susanne's hand.

Susanne stared at Henny. "Oh, I'm not worried,"

she said. "I know we'll be okay, especially if you're going to help us."

Henny tightened her grip on Susanne's hand. "We're going to go out on the *Gerda III*, Susanne—this time with you and your whole family. I said I'd take you sailing again."

At that, a smile crossed Susanne's face and she threw her arms around Henny. Henny returned the hug and then gently pulled Susanne's arms away.

Her last thought as she turned to leave was that this wasn't exactly the kind of outing she had had in mind.

CHAPTER 17

Otto and Gerhardt did not hesitate for one second when Henny told them what she was planning to do and asked for their help.

"I'm in," Otto said.

"Me too," added Gerhardt. "It's what we've been waiting for. We'll show those Nazis that they can't push us around!"

Henny could have cried. She wrapped her arms first around Otto and then around Gerhardt. "I knew I could count on the two of you," she said, muffled into Gerhardt's shoulder.

Henny couldn't remember another time when she had hugged these two. They were as formal and reserved as Far when it came to any demonstration of affection.

"Okay, okay," Gerhardt said, unwrapping her arms from around his neck and sniffling. "You're going to get me choked up in a minute." That, too, never happened!

They scheduled their test run for two days later. Otto had checked the weather reports and the conditions of the sea and determined that it would be a clear night, with just enough cloud cover to darken the sea and make it less likely for them to be spotted by other boats.

Henny hadn't said a word to her parents about the practice run, except to tell them that Otto and Gerhardt had agreed to come with her. Far told her that the key to Gerda was waiting for her at the pier whenever she needed it. He wasn't supposed to know exactly when she was going to take the boat out.

"If anything goes ... if anything happens," Henny said, "if anyone comes to question you, you won't have any information to give."

Far went pale when she explained this. But he didn't ask any questions. Still, he seemed to know when it was all going to take place, like he had a sixth sense. Or maybe it was Henny's heightened anxiety on that evening. She paced her bedroom like a cat in a cage, checking the time and glancing out the window at the darkening sky.

She planned to wait for her parents to go to bed before slipping out without being seen by them. Sure enough, at their usual bedtime, they said goodnight and went upstairs, and Henny prepared to leave. But just before she walked out the door, Far and Mor suddenly reappeared downstairs. Far reached out wordlessly and drew Henny into his arms, startling her completely. He squeezed her with all his might and held her there for what felt like an eternity.

Henny's breath caught in her throat. She reached up tentatively and returned the hug, standing in her father's embrace until he finally pulled away. "We've raised you right," he said, his voice thick with emotion. "Just be careful."

"Stay safe," Mor added, sniffling and pulling Henny over for a hug as well.

Henny couldn't talk. She knew she might break down completely if she tried to respond.

She walked quickly to the pier. The key was exactly where Far had said it would be. Otto and Gerhardt were already on board Gerda, preparing her to sail out into the channel. They were also stocking the hold with boxes of papers and supplies.

"I want us to be prepared," Otto explained. "If we're stopped on our way out into the channel, we can say we're taking supplies over to the lighthouse.

If we're stopped on our way back, we can say we're bringing back documents and other things from the lighthouse. Just trying to cover all the bases," he added.

Why hadn't she thought of that? It was another reason to be grateful that Otto and Gerhardt were included, though Henny hoped that no explanations would be needed, that they would be back here at the pier, safe and sound, before dawn. She carried the last of the boxes onto the boat and took them down the narrow staircase into the hold. Then, she entered the small cabin and took her place behind the wheel. She started up the motor and eased the boat away from the dock and into the channel.

The distance across to Sweden was only about fifteen miles—not that far—but in the dark, and in the choppy and unpredictable current, it could take several hours to get there. Henny pointed Gerda toward the coastline. Her destination was the Swedish port city of Limhamn, one of the closest sailing points from Copenhagen and the place she had sailed to on her one other trip to Sweden. Her route would take her north through Copenhagen harbor and out into the channel. Then she would sail toward the lighthouse just as she had always done with Far. From there, she would veer east toward Sweden.

Stars peeked out from behind the clouds scattered across the sky, shining more brightly whenever the moon made an appearance. Henny shuddered and pulled her jacket up around her neck. The mid-September weather was unpredictable at the best of times; on some days, it was still sweltering hot, as if summer had decided to stay indefinitely. On other days, it was cool and breezy. Tonight's air was on the chilly side and a cutting wind passed through Henny's jacket and into her skin. She felt completely on edge. And that made her tremble even more.

It's not that she wasn't sure of what she was doing. Rescuing her Jewish friends was the right thing to do—the only thing to do! Her resolve to complete this mission was stronger than ever. Still, her stomach was churning. It didn't help that the waves were getting stronger, pitching the *Gerda III* from side to side and up and down.

"Easy, girl," Henny whispered. "You've got a big job to do, and I need you to be as steady as possible."

As if Gerda had heard her, she suddenly evened out, steadying herself and moving more calmly through the water.

"That's it, Gerda," Henny said, smiling in the dark. "We can do this."

Otto and Gerhardt were at the bow of the boat,

eyes trained on the water, glancing back at Henny every now and then and shouting directions to her from their vantage point.

"Steer downwind. Now forward."

Henny followed their orders, steering the boat into the channel and toward the lights of Sweden that were blinking on the coastline ahead. Traffic on the channel was light, just a few fishing boats out on a nighttime run. And thankfully, there was no sign of any Nazi vessels. Henny hoped it would be as quiet and free of danger when she made this journey the next time, carrying Susanne and her family.

They passed the lighthouse with no problem, and on Otto's instruction, Henny turned the boat, leaving the lighthouse behind her, and began to sail into the more unfamiliar water. She knew that this was the most dangerous part of the journey. It was one thing to be stopped as she steered toward the lighthouse. But beyond that, there was no reason for her to be in open water.

Every muscle in Henny's body felt tight as she sailed forward across the channel. She finally looked at her watch and took a breath of relief as the pier of Limhamn came into view. She had made the crossing in just under three hours—better timing than she had thought!

She followed Otto's directions to steer toward a main docking station. She wasn't planning on stopping tonight. She just wanted to get as close to Limhamn as possible, then turn the boat around and take it back home. On the night of the actual mission, Henny imagined that there would be a group from the Swedish Resistance waiting with open arms to welcome the Rubin family. Tonight, it was quiet on shore. Henny brought Gerda up to the dock, then reversed the engine and backed her away, turning in a wide circle and then revving the engine once more to take Gerda back out into the channel.

As she sped away from Sweden, Henny felt elated. Everything had gone according to plan. The weather had remained cooperative, and most importantly, there had been no trouble. All the tension that she had been feeling earlier flowed out of her, replaced with a sense of confidence and strength that she could feel right in her bones. This was all easier than she had thought it would be. It *was* the perfect escape plan—she was sure of it! She was already beginning to think about the night to come, when she would make this journey with Susanne and her family on board.

They passed the lighthouse once more and Henny knew they were in the final stretch. Gerhardt, from his spot at the bow of the boat, turned to give her a thumbs-up. His face, even in the dark, looked as jubilant as Henny felt. His grin stretched from ear to ear. He looked like he was just about to shout something to her—probably some joke about how he could have crossed the channel faster than she had. But then his smile suddenly drained from his face, and his expression grew rigid.

She glanced over her shoulder to follow his gaze and saw a light trailing closely behind. A boat was on their tail, gaining speed and cutting the distance between itself and Gerda. And then she saw it—the Nazi flag with the swastika emblazoned on it flying from the boat's helm. A moment later, a megaphone boomed.

"Prepare to be boarded."

CHAPTER 18

Two soldiers stepped onto Gerda's deck, wearing the uniform of the Nazi army: high leather boots and a gray jacket cinched at the waist with a thick black belt. They held rifles that they had removed from their shoulders. They surveyed the boat, the barrels of their guns following their eyes, which moved from bow to stern, finally coming to rest on Henny, still standing behind the wheel. Otto and Gerhardt stood beside each other. Henny could see the loathing on her crewmembers' faces. One soldier marched up to Henny, his eyes staring steadily into hers.

"Give me your name."

He was young, Henny thought—not much older than she was, really just a boy dressing up and acting like a man. No, not a man, Henny checked herself, more like a bully and one with a lot of power.

"I'm Henny Sinding," she replied, her voice breaking. She was breathing fast and desperately trying to control her heart rate, which was threatening to gallop away from her. "This boat is the *Gerda III*, and this is my crew." *Breathe,* she commanded herself. *Don't show them that you're afraid.*

The young soldier did not break his stare. "And what are you doing out on the channel?"

The second soldier, just as young as the first, had moved to stand in front of Otto and Gerhardt. Otto lifted his head to watch Henny. His nostrils flared and his eyes narrowed. He looked as if he might pounce if anyone made a move to hurt her.

"Answer me," the first soldier repeated. "Why are you out here?"

"We've been taking supplies to the lighthouse," Henny replied, finding her voice again. Thank goodness Otto had stocked the hold with boxes. And thank goodness they were close to the lighthouse and not beyond it. The soldier didn't appear satisfied with her answer.

"It's rather late to be taking supplies across, isn't it?" he asked, shifting his rifle higher up on his shoulder.

Henny had to think fast. "We got a call from the

lighthouse for supplies. And they needed us to pick up a few things to return to the mainland. When the lighthouse calls, we answer, no matter when." Was that enough? Would that convince the soldiers to leave?

The soldier lowered his rifle and took a step closer. He reached into his pocket and drew out a small flashlight that he flicked on and then shone directly into Henny's face. She flinched and squinted into the piercing bright light.

"You're rather young to be doing this, aren't you?" he asked.

She could have said the same thing about him! Instead, she lifted her chin, trying to appear as calm and composed as possible.

"My father usually captains the Gerda, but he isn't feeling well. I've been sailing this boat for years." She had prepared for this question in advance of the test run. The less she said about Far, the better, she had reasoned. But there was no use hiding the fact that he owned the boat and usually did this work. Pretending that he was sick seemed like a valid excuse for his absence—at least she hoped so.

Another full minute passed while the young soldier continued to shine his flashlight into Henny's eyes. His partner was still focused on Otto and

Gerhardt. Even though the night air was cool, Henny could feel the sweat begin to gather across her forehead and the back of her neck. She didn't want to look scared, didn't want to give this soldier the pleasure of seeing her tremble and sweat.

"We've had reports that Jews may be trying to escape from Copenhagen." The soldier said the word *Jew* like something had gone bad in his mouth. "You wouldn't happen to know anything about that, would you?"

So, the Nazis knew of their plans! It took all of Henny's control to breathe deeply and evenly, to not react. "Of course not. As I said, we're just taking supplies back and forth from the lighthouse." *We've done nothing wrong*, she repeated in her mind—at least, nothing yet!

The soldier kept the flashlight in her face for one more minute before finally stepping back. "Hold the boat steady while I go below to inspect," he commanded. He pulled the door to the hold open, shone his flashlight inside, and then disappeared down the staircase.

The waves were starting to pick up, rolling under Henny's feet in long, rushing swells. She placed both hands on the steering wheel, trying to hold the boat steady. But as wave after wave rocked below her, another idea came to her. She locked eyes with Gerhardt. He nodded—a tiny movement of his head—and then reached out to hold onto the mast next to him. As if they had rehearsed, Otto grabbed the mast as well. Henny knew they were all thinking exactly the same thing. She gripped the steering wheel even harder and moved Gerda forward ever so slightly, all the while eyeing the waves that continued to rise and fall around her, each one bigger and bolder than the last. Then, with one more barely perceptible nod to Otto and Gerhardt, Henny wrenched the steering wheel to the left. Instead of navigating the boat through the approaching wave, Gerda hit the wave broadside, causing her to crest up over it and then rush down the other side. The boat pitched from side to side like a baby's cradle.

The rocking motion threw the soldier on deck off his feet. He yelped out loud and lurched forward, losing his grip on his rifle and frantically reaching out to grab at something to steady him. He missed the mast completely and staggered back, his arms swinging in wide circles.

The soldier from down below appeared at the top of the staircase, swaying back and forth on his feet like someone who'd had too much to drink. "I told you to keep the boat steady," he shouted, just as a second wave hit Gerda, taking her up and up to its peak and then smashing her down on the other side. Henny gripped the steering wheel for support while keeping an eye on Otto and Gerhardt, who continued to clutch at the mast with all their strength.

"I need to get off this boat before it kills me," the first soldier continued, grabbing for his rifle and launching himself off Gerda and back onto his boat, landing practically headfirst on the deck.

The second soldier clamored up to the gunnels. Before jumping off Gerda, he turned to face Henny. "Seems like you need some more practice to be able to captain this thing." Then he, too, jumped off, landing with a thud nearly on top of his partner. He regained his footing and turned once again to Henny. "I don't want to see you out on the water again," he shouted from his deck. "Do you understand?" A moment later, their boat roared away, leaving Henny and the Gerda in their wake.

As the boat sped away, Henny turned the wheel again, straightening Gerda out and holding her more evenly on the breakers. Her hands gripped the steering wheel, her breath rising and falling like the waves that had just surrounded them. No one spoke.

Finally, Otto turned to Henny, a wide smile on his face. "Genius!" he said.

"Did you see that soldier's face?" Gerhardt added. "Even in the dark, he looked as green as spinach."

Henny smiled weakly as relief swept over her, followed a moment later by a cold chill. This time, there had been nothing in the hold except for some boxes. And yet, the soldier had searched. Thanks to some quick thinking on her part, and the cooperation of the sea and Gerda, she had managed to get the Nazis off the boat quickly. What would happen the next time?

CHAPTER 19

By the time Henny crept back into the house, it was 3:00 a.m. She groaned, glancing at the clock, knowing she would still have to be up for school in the morning, and knowing that as much as she longed for sleep, thinking about the encounter with the Nazi soldiers on the channel would keep her awake. The fact that the Nazis had been patrolling at night and had followed and boarded Gerda was bad enough. But that they also knew Jewish citizens might be escaping on boats to Sweden was more disturbing than anything. She had to speak to the Resistance, to let them know what had happened to her and inform them that the Nazis might be onto any escape plan. Sleep eluded Henny. She tossed and turned, dozing for spurts before the sun finally lightened her room and she knew it was time to get up.

Far was waiting for her in the kitchen. He glanced at her face, her eyes ringed with shadows, and cautiously asked how the crossing had gone. Henny looked him straight in the eyes and replied, "Just as we planned. No problems at all."

He hesitated a moment, but then turned away, seeming to accept what she had said. Maybe he didn't want to know anything more than he needed to, and that was best for everyone.

Still, as jittery as she felt about the Nazi encounter, Henny knew that she needed to get the Rubin family out of Copenhagen as soon as possible. Was it her imagination or were there even more troops patrolling the streets of her city? She knew that any day now, the Nazis were going to begin arresting Jews across the country. There was no date when that roundup was going to start, at least none that she knew of. But she had to get the Rubin family to Sweden before the arrests began and all avenues for escape were cut off. The threat of that unknown date hung over her like a black cloud.

Henny was impatient; she didn't want another day to pass without helping her friends to safety. But everything was on hold, and not because of her. Astrid and Vincent had to coordinate with their resistance allies in Sweden, and that was taking more time than Henny had imagined.

"Just a few more days," Astrid said when Henny arrived at the resistance house later that day. When Henny told her about the practice run and the encounter with the Nazi boat, Astrid looked distressed. But she still wouldn't budge on the preparations. "You can't simply drop a Jewish family off on a dock on the other side. Someone has to be there to meet them, to take them to a safe place, to organize where they'll stay, and so much more." Henny understood all that, but still she itched to move forward with her plan.

In the meantime, and with Astrid's permission, she decided to ask Mr. Rubin to find another one or two Jewish families to come along with them whenever they got the okay to leave. She could probably take up to ten passengers in the hold. He agreed to discretely reach out in his community.

For the time being, all other late-night re-sistance activities continued to be suspended in the wake of the growing presence of Nazi soldiers on the streets, day and night. Henny went to school every day, pretending that things were normal. She said little to Lukas and the twins, except for brief passing comments in the schoolyard.

"Any word?" Henny would ask.

"Nothing," Lukas replied. "Have you heard anything?"

Henny would shake her head. "Why is it taking so long?"

A shrug and another shake of his head. "You know as much as we do."

Henny glanced over her shoulder during these quick exchanges. With more Nazis in the city, you never knew who might be eavesdropping. She was thinking mainly of Erik, though he seemed to have disappeared from school the last few days. She wondered briefly where he had gone, but realized how relieved she was not to see him lurking around corners. She tried to tell herself that he was harmless, aside from his few ridiculous comments about Jews. Still, he made her so jumpy, always popping up just after a conversation with one of her friends or skulking just around a corner.

When Henny arrived home from school one afternoon, nearly two weeks since her test run with Gerda, Far was waiting impatiently for her.

"We must talk," he said, pacing their hallway as though determined to wear out the carpet under his feet.

Henny's stomach shifted uneasily as she followed her father into the kitchen. Mor was already there, seated, hands folded in her lap. Her face was pale.

"What's wrong," Henny cried. "Are you okay?"

"We're fine," Mor replied, indicating that Henny should sit down.

Far took a deep breath before speaking. "I've heard that the roundup of Jewish citizens will happen the day after tomorrow, October first. Don't ask me too much," he added, holding his hand up to stop Henny from talking. "I also have connections in the city." He said that someone from his naval department had let him know that the Nazis were going to move through the city arresting Jews.

"Two days!" Henny repeated the ominous news in a whisper. After almost two weeks of waiting, this was all going to happen in two days.

"If you're going to take the Rubin family to safety, you have to do it now—tomorrow. It will be your last chance."

Henny swallowed hard and stared at her father. There was so much to do, so much to think about. Would Susanne and her family be ready to go by tomorrow? Would Astrid have secured all the plans in Sweden? Would the weather cooperate? On and on, the questions circled round her mind. After all this time of waiting and wondering, it suddenly felt as if there was no time to prepare.

"Are you sure you don't want me to come with you?" Far asked. "I'm ..." He hesitated and pointed to Mor. "*We're* prepared to help in any way we can."

Henny smiled at them gratefully. "I know you are. Both of you." It was bad enough that her parents knew when she was going to sail. They were already implicated in more ways than she had wanted. "I appreciate everything you've ever done for me. But we'll manage this: Otto, Gerhardt, and me. We know what we're doing."

She didn't feel nearly as certain as those words she spoke aloud.

After talking with her parents, Henny made a beeline for the safe house of her resistance group. Getting there was trickier than ever. In the last few days, the Nazis had instituted a curfew, another sign that they were now fully in charge. All residents of Copenhagen had to be off the street by eight o'clock. Henny dove behind buildings and statues each time she heard a car approach or thought she heard the clomping of soldiers' boots on the pavement, warning her that a Nazi patrol might be approaching. She was turning one last corner before arriving on the street of the familiar gray door when she nearly ran headlong into Lukas!

"You scared me to death!" Henny cried, coming to an abrupt stop and pushing Lukas back against a stone wall, her heart thumping wildly in her chest. "I was coming to the safe house to tell everyone—"

"We know." Lukas stopped her, holding his hand up in the air. "The roundup is happening in two days."

"How—?"

"Astrid and Vincent told us. They sent me out to get you."

Of course, Astrid and Vincent would have this information through their own sources. Henny wouldn't have to explain anything to them. She and Lukas ran the last block to the resistance house and tapped out the coded entry signal. Astrid and Vincent and several others were gathered around a map of the channel between Denmark and Sweden. Henny's route from Copenhagen to Limhamn was already drawn on the map.

"We're trying to secure a number of boats besides yours to carry Jewish families across the channel," Astrid said.

"It's the start of what we hope will be a mass

evacuation," added Vincent.

"Everything's been arranged in Limhamn. Sweden is ready. It's time," Astrid said.

"And there's one more thing you need to know," Lukas piped up. "I'm going to go with you."

"To Sweden?" Henny asked.

"All the way across. It's been a while since I've been sailing. So, you may have to bring me up to speed," he added, smiling. Henny didn't respond. She wasn't sure what she thought about the notion of Lukas going with her, especially as he wasn't an experienced sailor. She already had the help of Otto and Gerhardt. Lukas might slow them down.

"Everyone has a role in this escape plan," he said, noting her hesitation.

She smiled briefly. Even with Otto and Gerhardt, perhaps she could use the extra pair of hands, especially if she was going to take more than one family across the channel.

"I guess this way, I'll get to order you around," she finally replied.

CHAPTER 20

Later that night, Mr. Rubin answered the door so quickly that it was as if he were waiting for Henny's knock. When she told him that the Nazis were planning to round up the Jews of the city in two days, his face grew dark.

"Yes, our rabbi has warned us. He stopped the prayers in synagogue today to tell us that the Nazis had the names and addresses of every Jew in Denmark. They're coming for us. Two days from now." He looked over at Henny. "Did you know that October first is the Jewish New Year? One of the holiest days for our community."

Henny hadn't known that. She shook her head.

"The Nazis must know that we'll be gathered with our families on that day, in our homes celebrating together. No adult will be at work. No child will be at school. The Nazis won't need to look very hard to find us. It'll be as easy as shooting fish in a barrel," he added bitterly.

Henny felt his anger and she shared in it.

"I have another two families ready to come with us," Mr. Rubin said. "Four adults and two children. Just tell us where and when."

"We'll leave tomorrow," Henny said. "I'll come for your family just after dark, and we'll go to the pier together."

On the following evening, September 30, just before dark, Henny slipped out of her house again and walked over to the Rubins'. Her parents had retreated upstairs early. They knew where Henny was going. But clearly, they did not want to watch their daughter walk out the door. She knew how worried they must have been. She was relieved not to have to see it written on their faces.

Henny was just as anxious. She hadn't been able to think straight all day. She had put her stockings on the wrong feet and made a second cup of tea for herself before she had even taken a sip of the first one! Even now, her hands were shaking as she pulled her hair back off her face and tucked it under a dark cap. She needed to calm down. For one thing, she couldn't show the Rubins, especially Susanne, how scared she was. They were all putting their trust in her and she needed to be strong and confident for them. And besides that, she needed to have all her wits about her when she made the crossing. Any distractions could prove disastrous.

The Rubin family was already waiting in the hallway of their home when Henny arrived, all except Aron, who ran back and forth between the hallway and dining room, giggling like any two-year-old about to go on a journey. She greeted everyone and then reached down to tuck Susanne's scarf into her jacket. Mrs. Rubin had plaited Susanne's hair into two long braids that Henny tucked under Susanne's hat.

"It's a bit cold out there," she said, trying to keep her voice calm and her hands steady. "You'll need to keep your jacket buttoned up." Then she paused and looked Susanne in the eye. Susanne looked relaxed and untroubled. Her eyes were filled with more trust than Henny had ever seen.

And then Susanne reached her hand out and stroked Henny's cheek. "We're going to be fine," she said.

Henny couldn't reply; she was completely taken

aback by Susanne's composure. Somehow, it gave Henny strength. She nodded and stood up.

She went over the plan with the Rubins. She would escort them to the boat. She had arranged for Lukas to bring the other Jewish families that Mr. Rubin knew. They would all assemble at an abandoned warehouse close to the pier, before boarding Gerda.

"Depending on conditions on the water, it shouldn't take more than three hours to get across to Sweden," Henny added. "And you'll be met on the other side by some people who will help you get settled there." She knew so little about this part of the plan. Astrid and Vincent had taken care of those details and assured her that all was in place for the arrival of the families. Mr. and Mrs. Rubin didn't ask a single question. They just stared at Henny, nodding from time to time as she explained everything. They looked overwhelmed by it all, their faces pasty, their eyes wide and slightly unfocused.

Then, Henny reached into her coat pocket and pulled out a very small folded-over square of paper. She unwrapped it carefully to reveal a tiny pill.

"You need to give this to Aron," she said, handing the pill to Mrs. Rubin. Aron was still whooping at the top of his lungs. "It'll make him sleep, and we need him to be still and quiet during the crossing."

Mrs. Rubin gulped and nodded. She caught Aron as he ran past them and took him to their kitchen. When she returned a few minutes later, he was in her arms, awake but quiet. "It's done," she said. Henny didn't ask how she had managed to get the pill into him.

"It's time to go," she said, letting her gaze sweep across the Rubin family.

Mr. Rubin picked up a small bag and reached for his wife's arm. "I don't know how we can ever begin to thank you for everything you are doing for us," he said to Henny. "We are forever in your debt."

"Please, don't," Henny interrupted. "Getting you safely to Sweden is all the thanks I want."

With that, she opened the door, then glanced up and down the street. With the family following close behind, Henny took Susanne's hand and left the house.

CHAPTER 21

Henny led the way to the pier, keeping the family close to the shops, trees, and statues that lined the road next to the channel. Once, she heard a motorcar approaching from behind. She thought it might be a Nazi patrol and she quickly steered the family behind a building, pressing against the wall with Susanne's hand tightly in hers. Mrs. Rubin had given Aron over to her husband. The baby's head was nestled against Mr. Rubin's shoulder, his eyes closed, his breathing even. The pill had done its work and Henny hoped that Aron would stay quiet for the entire journey.

They continued to hug the building wall as the sound of the car engine came closer and closer. The wide beam of a headlight passed by, illuminating the road ahead. Henny held her breath as a dark car rolled past, belching black smoke from its exhaust. She closed her eyes tightly, not wanting to know what kind of car it was, or who might be behind the wheel.

"You're squeezing my hand too hard," Susanne whispered as the car drove on into the night.

"Sorry!" Henny loosened her grip. Then, she peeked out at the road, checking in both directions for vehicles. All was quiet and clear.

"Let's keep moving," Henny whispered, starting out again, the family close behind her. She quickened the pace, and as darkness settled firmly on the city, they arrived at the pier and headed directly to the abandoned warehouse. The Resistance had checked it out beforehand to be sure that it was empty, making it a perfect place for Henny's group to meet and prepare for the crossing. Lukas was already inside when Henny and the Rubins entered by a storage room at the back of the building. With him were several other people.

Before Henny could even say a word, Mr. Rubin ran forward and clasped the hand of one of the gentlemen who stood next to Lukas.

"These are our friends," he said, turning back to Henny. "This is Mr. and Mrs. Meyer and their children, Raquel and Martin. And these are Mrs. Meyer's parents, Mr. and Mrs. Hertz. We've known them for years. Our children are friends as well."

Henny shook hands all around and surveyed her passengers. Six adults and four children. It would be a tight squeeze inside the hold of the *Gerda III*.

Mr. and Mrs. Meyer each grasped one of Henny's hands. "You are an angel," Mrs. Meyer said. Her voice shook with emotion. "Thank you for saving our lives—my husband, my parents, my children." Their daughter, Raquel, looked to be about Susanne's age, with the same dark hair and round eyes. They could have been sisters. And Martin, as young as Aron, was already fast asleep in his father's arms. Henny confirmed with Lukas that he had given the family a sedative for their little boy. Aron's head still rested heavily on Mr. Rubin's shoulder. Henny prayed again that the pills would work their magic long enough to get them across to Sweden and safety.

Mrs. Meyer's parents, Mr. and Mrs. Hertz, were older. They stood slightly behind the others, arms intertwined, propped up against each other as if neither would be able to stand on their own. Mr. Hertz also carried a wooden cane. Would they be able to manage the crossing? Henny wondered with some concern. Would they even be able to climb down the small staircase into the hold?

"I used to sail a bit myself," Mr. Hertz said, as if

reading Henny's mind. "My wife and I have been on many boats. You don't have to worry about us." Then he pointed at his cane and chuckled slightly. "This old thing is just for show. And besides, I can use it to knock over any Nazi that might get in my way." He thrust the cane out in front of himself like a sword.

Henny smiled gratefully at him and then gathered everyone together in front of her. "You're all going to wait here for a little while. I'm going to go over to my boat and check in with my crew. Then I'll come back and begin to move you all onto the *Gerda III* and into the hold. That's where you'll stay for the crossing. In the meantime, find a place to sit and try to rest for a little bit, if you can. We have some sandwiches for you, so eat something. I'll let you know when it's time to go."

The families began to settle against the wall. Henny noted that Susanne had taken Raquel by the hand and was sitting with her, talking about what it was like to sail on the Gerda. "She can go as fast or as slow as you want," Susanne was saying. "I even know how to steer her. And you have to remember that Gerda is a *she*."

Henny turned to Lukas. "Any trouble getting here?" she asked. He shook his head. Then she noticed the rifle resting at his side.

"Something we took from the Nazis in one of our raids," he said. "It's just a precaution."

She nodded. "Okay, stay with the families. I need to make sure everything is set to go on board."

As Lukas nodded in the dim light of the warehouse, Henny realized that this was her mission now. Lukas had led her through many late-night excursions. He had told her where to go, taught her how to distribute pamphlets, and steered her out of several tricky and dangerous situations. She had followed his lead, listening to him and trusting his decisions. But now, she was the one in charge, and Lukas knew it.

As though he'd read her mind, he raised his hand to his forehead and declared, "Aye aye, Captain!"

Chapter 22

Otto and Gerhardt were loading supplies onto the boat when Henny approached.

"We're nearly ready to go," Otto said. "Everything good in there?" He nodded his head toward the warehouse.

"Everything's all set," Henny replied, grabbing a box from the pier and bringing it on board. "We've got ten passengers: six adults and four little ones. So, we're going to have to figure out how many boxes we can bring with us."

As in the test run two weeks before, they were going to be carrying supplies inside the hold. The plan was to load the families in first and then pile boxes up against the door so that these would be the first things anyone would see if they were to inspect inside. Hopefully, the cargo would deter a patrol group from checking further. Henny prayed none of that would happen, and that all of this was just added precaution. Using the supply boxes as a decoy had been Gerhardt's idea.

Gerhardt often had great ideas. But his next one took Henny by surprise. He grabbed one of the last boxes from the pier and jumped onto the boat, holding it tightly. When Henny came near, the smell from inside the box nearly knocked her off her feet.

"What is that?" she exclaimed, holding her nose and flinching.

Gerhardt smiled broadly. "Fish! Herring, to be precise. They've been sitting here on the dock for most of the day, so the smell is at its peak. I figure no one is going to want to inspect the hold too closely if we put this box inside."

Henny grinned. "It's brilliant! Now, let's just hope the families don't get sick when they're cooped up underneath the deck with this close by."

Henny watched as Gerhardt loaded the box of fish on board Gerda. She glanced up, drew the collar of her jacket higher around her neck, and pulled her cap further down on her forehead. Gentle drops of rain were falling from a cloud-drenched sky. A light fog had rolled in from the sea beyond the channel.

The cloud cover and fog were good, Henny figured; the less chance of Gerda being seen on the crossing, the better. But the fog would also make it more difficult for her to steer the boat. And the rain would make the water choppier and the journey more hazardous. She hoped the rain wouldn't get harder, but there was nothing she could do about it. There was no use fretting, she told herself. She had other things to worry about, like getting the families on board, hiding them, and pushing off.

She checked one more time to make sure everything she needed was there: life jackets, extra oars, enough gas in the tank, sails tightly secured. Then, Henny stood before Otto and Gerhardt.

"I don't know if I've told you how thankful I am that you're coming with me," she began.

Otto raised his hand. "Henny, stop," he said. "We wanted a way to fight back and you've given us this chance to do something meaningful."

"We're proud of who you've grown up to be," Gerhardt added. "And proud to stand by your side."

Henny's eyes glistened as she stared back at them. Before leaving the boat to go back to the warehouse, she paused, laying her hand on one of the wooden gunnels.

"Well, this is it, Gerda," she whispered into the

darkness. "I'm counting on you to help a lot of wonderful people tonight. Are you ready?" The boat rocked gently from side to side as if nodding *yes. Daring and brave,* Henny thought to herself. In the past weeks, she had become both. And now, her courage and nerve would be put to the test one more time. "I know you can do this, Gerda," Henny added. "I'm here for you too. So, let's get the job done, together."

Lukas and the families were waiting for her when she reentered the warehouse. It didn't look as if anyone had rested while she had been checking the boat. And most of the food was untouched. The adults paced nervously, while Susanne and her friend Raquel continued to hold hands and whisper together. Only the babies, held by their fathers, slept soundlessly as if they didn't have a care in the world.

"I'd like you to gather your things and move to the door," Henny instructed. "Then, Lukas and I will walk you across the pier to the boat. Stay as quiet as you can. Walk quickly and be alert. If you see anything out of the ordinary, let me know immediately." She paused and looked around. Mrs. Rubin and Mrs. Meyer looked pale, even in the dim light of the warehouse. Mr. Rubin and Mr. Meyer nodded gravely. The elderly Mr. and Mr. Hertz continued to clutch one another in what looked like a white-knuckle grip.

Henny took a deep breath and continued. "My crew will get you on board and help you into the hold, where you'll stay for the entire journey. Follow their instructions. It's going to be a tight squeeze once you're inside. But I know you'll manage. And just remember that in a few hours, you'll all be safely in Sweden." She said this with as much hope in her voice as she could muster.

Everyone nodded solemnly. Before leaving, Mr. Rubin stepped forward.

"May I just say again, on behalf of everyone here, how grateful we all are to you, Henny, and to you, Lukas, and to everyone who has planned our escape."

"There'll be plenty of time for thanks later," Henny replied. "Now, let's get you all on the boat and get going."

They walked in a line, led by Henny, with Lukas in the rear. At the door of the warehouse, Henny raised her hand and the group behind her shuffled to a stop. Then, she opened the door slowly and glanced outside. The sight that greeted her made her stomach plunge.

Two Nazi soldiers were standing on the pier, right in front of the *Gerda III*, blocking the path between the warehouse and the boat. They had appeared out of nowhere and now stood back to back, rifles up against their shoulders, as though waiting for something. Thankfully, Otto and Gerhardt were nowhere to be seen. They must have gone into the cabin of the boat, Henny thought. She was sure they were watching the soldiers just as she was.

She froze. Quickly, she ducked her head back inside. Lukas was by her side in an instant.

"What is it?"

Henny motioned out the door. Lukas cracked it open, glanced outside, and then quickly shut it. He looked at her, shaking his head from side to side.

Henny took another deep breath and faced the families. "There's a bit of a ... delay," she began. She told them about the soldiers. "We just have to wait here for a few minutes and see what they're going to do. I'm sure they'll move on shortly, and then we can get on board."

She hoped that would be the case, though a sickening feeling was rising up inside of her. What if the soldiers didn't move on? What if they had come to inspect the warehouse?

Mrs. Rubin looked as if she might pass out. A muscle twitched at the corner of her right eye, and her mouth formed a tight line. She looked over at her husband, who looked equally afraid. Susanne walked over to Henny and tugged on her arm.

"Are we ready to leave yet?" she asked when Henny had turned to face her.

"Soon," Henny replied. "We're almost ready to go. Thank you for watching out for Raquel," she added. "You're such a good friend and a good helper, keeping her calm."

Susanne nodded. "I can do so many things to help you, can't I?"

Oh, if only she could make the soldiers disappear, Henny thought, as she smiled and nodded at Susanne. Henny could feel her pulse pounding in her temples as she turned to look out the door once more.

The soldiers were still there, standing back to back. But as Henny watched, one of them gave a loud command. Both snapped to attention, and then began to walk away from one another in opposite directions. Henny braced herself. What was happening? Were they leaving? This was too good to be true.

She followed the path they were taking away from one another, and away from the pier. The fog was still hanging in the air, and as the soldiers marched away, their forms faded in the mist. They had each gone about one hundred paces and Henny was just about to announce that the coast was once again clear when suddenly, the same soldier shouted another command, more loudly this time, as he was some distance from his comrade. Both soldiers stopped, turned, and began to march back toward one another. They met at the exact spot where they had started. And then the whole sequence began again: standing back to back, marching away, turning, and walking toward one another.

Henny's heart was sinking fast. And just when she thought it couldn't get any worse, she caught a glimpse of the face of one of the soldiers. And that was when she knew they were doomed.

CHAPTER 23

It was Erik! There he was in a Nazi uniform, holding a rifle and parading back and forth, right in front of the *Gerda III* and right in front of Henny. It all made sense now: his secrecy, the way he suddenly appeared right when she was in the middle of a conversation with Lukas, not to mention his recent comments about Jews.

She gasped and Lukas was by her side again. Henny pointed out the door and felt Lukas stiffen.

"Traitor!" he whispered, his voice trembling with anger.

Henny needed to think and think fast. She watched as Erik and his partner marched back and forth several more times, hoping each time that they would continue to stomp away and not return.

That wasn't the case. They were not going anywhere. They had chosen this spot to patrol back and forth, and they were not going to leave.

What if Erik and his partner were here for the night? What if they continued to patrol until daybreak? Any chance of escape would be lost. Tomorrow was October 1, the day the Nazis would sweep through the city, arresting all Jewish families.

She glanced up again at the sky. The fog still hung in the air, a light rain continued to fall—perfect conditions for the journey. It couldn't possibly all end here, she thought desperately, not after everything she had planned and not after promising Susanne and the other families that she would get them to safety. There had to be a way out of this, if only she could think of it.

She continued to watch the soldiers march back and forth, silently counting the steps they took to reach their furthermost spot, turn, and march back. It was one hundred steps in each direction, each and every time.

"Lukas, listen to me!" she whispered. "I think there may be a way around this. And it may be our only chance."

"Tell me!" he declared.

"They march away from each other for one

hundred paces before turning back. Our only chance to get these families across the pier and onto the boat is during those one hundred steps, when those two have their backs turned." She still had to figure out how to start Gerda's engine and get her away from the pier without attracting attention. But if she had the families on board, perhaps they could just make a run for it and hope for the best.

It was risky, for sure. The soldiers could change their pattern, they might suddenly turn around mid-march, or one of their group could make a noise and bring the soldiers running. Any number of things could go wrong. But what choice did they have? Tomorrow the roundups would begin. It was now or never.

"The timing is going to have to be perfect," Lukas said.

Henny nodded. "And we can't do this in one big group. We're going to have to take turns, you and I going with a pair, and then returning for another."

Lukas and Henny continued to talk out the fine points; one of them would stay with the families while the other took two over to the boat. That way, if anything went wrong, at least someone would be there with the remaining family members and hopefully keep them safe. Henny needed to figure out who would go with whom and in what order. Once they were satisfied that they had covered all the details and could do this, Henny turned back to the families, who were still waiting soundlessly in a huddle behind her. She explained as calmly as she could the situation and the plan.

"I don't know about this," Mr. Rubin began, looking at his wife and children. "We have the little ones, and then there's Mr. and Mrs. Hertz ..."

His voice trailed off, but Henny knew what he was thinking. It would be dangerous enough for the grown-ups to run across the pier with the Nazi soldiers so close. But how would the children manage? And how could the elderly couple be expected to sprint to the Gerda like two racers?

Mr. Hertz tapped his cane firmly on the floor of the warehouse. "Please, do not underestimate my wife and me. We can do anything that is asked of us," he said confidently. "Just lead the way!"

Henny glanced at Mr. Rubin and then nodded at the group. "Okay," she said. "I'm going to start with Mr. Hertz and Mrs. Meyer. You're coming with me first." She figured that, as strong as Mr. Hertz claimed he and his wife were, it would be better to split up the elderly couple and pair them each with someone who could help them get across the pier as quickly as possible.

Just before turning to the door, Henny felt a tug on her jacket. It was Susanne.

"Don't leave me," she begged. The fear in her eyes nearly broke Henny's heart. All the boldness that Henny had always seen in her little friend seemed to have disappeared.

Henny bent toward her. "I'm just taking some of the others to the Gerda first. And then it'll be your turn. I'm not leaving you. I promise. I just need you to stay here for a few more minutes with Raquel. Can you do that?"

Susanne blinked rapidly, tears collecting in her eyes. Finally, she nodded solemnly. Henny squeezed her hand tightly before straightening up. She glanced out the door, waiting until Erik and his partner were at their starting position in front of Gerda and had begun to march away from one another. She counted to ten, then took Mr. Hertz's cane and grabbed him by his one arm, while Mrs. Meyer took his other arm. They walked out the door of the warehouse, moving swiftly across the pier. At one point, she could feel Mr. Hertz slipping on the wet cobblestones. She tightened her grip on his arm, pulling him along until his feet barely touched the ground.

Out of the corner of her eye, she could see Erik, his back to her, still marching away. She realized she had lost count. Would they get to the boat before Erik turned back? Mrs. Meyer was breathing heavily on the other side of Mr. Hertz, and Henny prayed that the thick fog would muffle the sound. Gerda was just ahead of them; twenty more steps, then ten, then five, and finally they were by her side.

Otto and Gerhardt appeared as if Henny had summoned them. They jumped off the boat silently, and each grabbed an arm of one of the two passengers. Then, they helped Mr. Hertz and Mrs. Meyer on board and quickly led them down the stairs and into the hold. Henny jumped on board as well. She ducked into the cabin and waited there while Erik and his partner returned to their starting point. It was only when they began to march away from one another again that Henny sprinted back across the pier and into the warehouse.

She was breathing hard when she entered, partly from the dash across the pier and partly from the adrenaline rushing through her body like a giant wave. But she had done it! The first two passengers were on board.

It was Lukas's turn to take two more family members, while Henny stayed with the others. He motioned for Mrs. Hertz to stand next to him, with Mrs. Rubin on her other side. Henny watched out the door and gave them the all clear once the two soldiers had begun to march away from one another. Lukas and the two women ran out the door. He reappeared minutes later and gave Henny a thumbs-up.

Next to go was Mr. Rubin, holding baby Aron, still fast asleep in his arms. Henny ran them across the pier, returning a few minutes later. Lukas then went with Mr. Meyer holding baby Martin in his arms. Finally, it was just Susanne and Raquel.

"I'll take Raquel and wait on board. When the coast is clear, you bring Susanne," Lukas said.

He took Raquel by the hand when Henny stopped him. "Lukas, you've helped enough. But I need to take it from here. I don't want you coming with me," she said, keeping her voice low so that the two little girls wouldn't hear.

"What are you talking about? We agreed—"

"We've lost so much time," Henny interrupted. They were now on a deadline; they needed to leave without any more delays. If not, she feared that the little ones might wake up and start to cry. That could give them all away in an instant. The weather might get worse, making the crossing more difficult, or even impossible! The traffic on the channel could get busier as light approached, arousing suspicion as Gerda sailed past the lighthouse. If they were caught, how would she ever be able to explain Lukas's presence on board? But above all, she was the one responsible for the passengers, and every minute of delay weighed heavily on her. "I can't have an inexperienced sailor on the boat," Henny said. "Things have to move quickly now. I can't stop to explain things to you."

"I won't get in the way," Lukas insisted. "I'm there to help protect you—and the other families," he added, patting the rifle he carried in his other hand.

"It's not that I don't appreciate it. I do. It's just ..." She hesitated. Lukas needed to understand that his presence might increase the danger. She needed to complete this mission on her own—on her terms, in her way.

Lukas reached out to take Henny's arm. "Please, listen to me," he began. "I'm the one who introduced you to the Resistance. I'm the one who went with you night after night to plaster buildings with pamphlets. I need to see this through to the end with you, to help take these families to freedom. We're a team, Henny."

Henny felt a soft tug on her jacket. Susanne was standing next to her, looking up. "Are we going yet?" she asked.

Henny closed her eyes. When she opened them, Lukas was staring at her. "From start to finish," he said.

Henny let out a shaky breath. "Okay. We'll do this together."

Lukas took Raquel by the hand and moved to the door. A quick glance outside, and then the two of them were gone. Henny looked down at Susanne, her eyes solemn in the low light of the warehouse.

"We're going to be fine," Henny said. "Just stay close to me, and we'll be on the Gerda before you know it."

Susanne dropped her head. Henny leaned toward her, and when she was close, Susanne suddenly threw her arms around Henny's neck, hugging her with all her might. Tears gathered in Henny's eyes. She returned Susanne's hug, then gently pried her arms away from her neck. Finally, she stood, grabbed Susanne's hand, and moved to the door.

"Let's get you on the boat," she said.

CHAPTER 24

Henny checked the positions of Erik and his partner, and when they were marching away from one another, she dashed across the pier with Susanne next to her. They made it with no trouble. Otto was there to lift Susanne onto the boat and Henny quickly followed. Once on board, Henny climbed down the small staircase into the hold and pulled Susanne down after her. Mrs. Rubin's face erupted in relief when her daughter appeared. She grabbed her and enfolded her into a big hug.

"Thank goodness," she muttered, stroking Susanne's hair. "We're all together now. That's what's most important."

Henny surveyed her group of passengers. They were huddled together in a corner of the hold, stooped over so their heads wouldn't hit the low wooden beams above them. Their faces were strained and tired. Henny shared the exhaustion that they must have been feeling. But there was no time to rest or let down her guard. They were not out of the woods yet.

"Find a seat somewhere on the floor," she whispered. "You have to stay as far away from this staircase and the door as you possibly can." She explained to them that she and her crewmates were going to start piling boxes and supplies in front of them and all the way up the stairs. "It's going to get stuffy in here. Hopefully, this won't be for too long," she added.

"We can manage," Mr. Rubin said.

"You'll have enough air coming through the cracks in the wood to be able to breathe properly. But it also means that you can't make a sound while you're down here. You'll be able to hear us above you. Remember, if you can hear us, we can probably hear you. So, not a whisper, not a cough, not a cry." She glanced at the babies still sleeping against their fathers' shoulders.

"We understand what we must do," said Mr. Hertz.

"Lukas is going to stay down here with you, for extra protection," Henny said, staring evenly at Lukas. She still worried that if the Nazis decided to board the boat, it would be difficult to explain his presence—an extra person on deck at night with little sailing experience.

He lifted his rifle. "That's right. And I'm not afraid to use this if I have to."

With that, Lukas took his place next to the passengers.

Henny called up softly to Otto and Gerhardt to start handing boxes down to her. She placed them at the feet of the passengers, who had taken spots on the floor at the far end of the hold. Then, she began to pile the boxes up until, before long, there was a mountain of them blocking the Jewish families. Lukas's face, grim and determined, was the last face she saw before placing the final box on top of the pile. Then, she backed up the steps, adding boxes on each one. The last one to go in the hold was the box of fish. It seemed as if the disgusting smell had gotten even worse in the time it had taken to load the families on board Gerda. The fumes began to waft down the stairs. From down below, she could hear Mrs. Rubin begin to cough.

"I'm so sorry," Henny whispered. "It's just another precaution. Are you all okay?"

"We'll be fine," Mr. Rubin replied hoarsely. "It will just take a moment to adjust."

Mrs. Rubin stifled another cough, and then all

was silent. Henny climbed out of the hold and closed the door tightly behind her, locking it with a padlock that Otto handed to her and depositing the key in her pocket. She piled blankets, life jackets, oars, and rope over the door, adding yet another barrier between them and their precious cargo below.

"Are we really going to be able to do this?" she asked Gerhardt, a moment of doubt seeping into her mind.

"It's as good as done," he replied firmly. "The hard part is over. It's time to go."

Henny gave a silent prayer that Gerhardt was right, and then she glanced at her watch. With the delay in getting the families on board, it was much later than she had planned, and all her fears about the little ones waking, the weather, and the traffic on the channel were pounding through her mind. On top of that, she was worried that if she didn't get these families to Sweden in the next few hours, the Resistance group waiting for them on the other side might give up and leave. Then what would her families do? She couldn't abandon them there with no one to help them. The clock was ticking, and she had to get out of there fast. But there was still one big problem.

Henny looked back at the pier and spotted Erik and his partner marching back to their starting point in front of Gerda. Quickly, she ducked her head and indicated for Otto and Gerhardt to do the same. How were they going to start up the boat and get away from the pier without being heard? And then, an idea came to her.

"Otto," she whispered. "As soon as those two begin to march away from each other, you and I are going to jump off the boat and run to the warehouse. Gerhardt, you stay here."

"But why?" Otto asked.

She shook her head. No time to explain. "Just trust me and follow my lead."

Silently, she watched until the two soldiers had turned away from each other and the boat. Then, she pulled Otto by the arm, and together they jumped onto the dock and scurried across the pier to the warehouse. They stayed in the shadows until Erik and his partner were beginning to march back in their direction. And then, Henny pulled Otto by the arm once more and began to stroll across the pier. Her voice echoed loudly in the dark.

"I can't believe we have to make another run tonight," she called out. "I wish those men at the lighthouse would get their supply order right so we don't need to keep going back and forth."

The only way to escape suspicion, Henny reasoned, was to make herself noticeable, to show that she had nothing to hide. That was her plan, plain and simple. She would let the soldiers know that she was taking Gerda out for a routine run. If they questioned her, hopefully they would accept her explanation and let her pass. At first, Otto's eyes grew wide as Henny dragged him along. She stared at him, praying silently that he would understand. And then, he nodded and grinned in the dark.

"It's not the first time we've had to go out so late, and it won't be the last," he replied loudly.

They reached Gerda and were just about to jump on board when suddenly, a bright spotlight flooded across the dock. A moment later, a voice boomed out in the dark.

"Halt!"

Henny and Otto froze, the light nearly blinding her. She reached up to shield her eyes, trying to look past the light, knowing exactly who was shouting the order. But the intense spotlight remained fixed on her face. A moment later, Erik and his partner came to a stop in front of her. Erik looked at Henny and then over at Otto. A slow smile spread across his face as he switched off the light and stepped forward.

"Hello, Henny," he said. "Kind of late for a boat ride, isn't it?"

Chapter 25

Henny was struggling to see clearly. Even with the light turned off, blotches of black swam like dark bubbles before her eyes.

"What are you doing out here, Erik?" She blinked and reached up to rub her eyes. Erik's face slowly came into focus when she reopened them.

He frowned. "Perhaps you can answer me instead. Why are *you* out here?"

"We're taking supplies over to the lighthouse."

Erik glanced at his watch. "At this hour?"

Henny's plan, which had seemed so reasonable to her a moment earlier, suddenly felt ridiculous. There was no way Erik and his partner were going to buy into this. "We had a call that the staff out there was low on some essential items," she replied, struggling to calm her voice. "My father usually does the late run, but he hasn't been feeling well lately. So, I offered to do it instead." That reason had done the trick on her test run, and she prayed it would work now.

Erik paused, seeming to consider what Henny had said. Then, he looked over at Otto. "And you? What's your reason for being out here?"

Otto's eyes were narrowed, hard and cold, staring at Erik with a burning hatred. Henny's heart hammered. She was afraid that his anger was about to get the better of him and that he would say or do something rash. She knew she had to try to diffuse the situation, to back him away from a confrontation rather than let him engage in it. If not, they would have an even bigger problem on their hands.

"This is one of my crewmembers," she said, jumping in before Otto could say or do anything. "He helps me on all of my runs. My other crewmember is already on board." She pointed up at Gerhardt, who appeared on deck looking as hostile as Otto.

"And we have to get going quickly," Henny added. "I've got to get back and try to get some sleep. I've got *school* tomorrow." She emphasized the word. "By the way, I've missed you in class."

Erik paused, eyeing her and Otto. "Who needs school when there's so much more important work to do. My father got me this position. I'm helping protect the city now."

Protect the city? The only thing we need protection from is people like you, Henny thought angrily. But before she could reply, Otto began to talk.

"Impressive," he said. "The Nazis are so lucky to have you."

Could Erik detect Otto's oozing sarcasm? Henny guessed not. Erik puffed out his chest and smiled broadly.

"My father says that Hitler will do great things for Denmark, just as he has done for other countries across Europe."

Henny swallowed her own anger. All she could think about were the families huddled together in the hold. She wondered if they could hear everything that was happening on shore. She figured they must be scared out of their minds. And she was terrified along with them, worrying above all else that Mrs. Rubin might cough, or Aron might wake up and cry, or Mr. Hertz might shift position and knock into something. The sound would travel up to the deck and out onto the pier, and they would all be doomed. Each moment that ticked away was a moment that increased the danger for them—for all of them!

"Yes, well, I need to get out on the water," Henny

said again. "We've got work to do."

A moment that felt eternal passed. Finally, Erik smiled and stepped back. "All right," he said. "Move on."

Henny almost couldn't believe what she was hearing. Her plan had worked. And now, she was going to be able to sail Gerda away with no interference from Erik or his partner.

She didn't hesitate for another moment. She nodded at Otto who began to untie Gerda from the dock. Henny joined him, bending to grab the ropes.

"That was brilliant," he murmured.

"I just want to get out of here," she whispered.

Finally, she jumped on board, moved into the cabin, and took her place behind the wheel. She inserted the key into the ignition and listened to the pop, pop, pop of the engine as it came to life. She was just about to begin easing the boat away from the pier when the spotlight flooded across the deck of Gerda and came to rest again on Henny.

"Wait!" This command came from Erik's partner. Up until now, he hadn't said a word. "Turn off the boat and stop what you're doing!"

Henny turned off the engine and stepped out of the cabin. The light followed her on to the deck where Gerhardt was standing and squinting down at the pier. Otto was still on shore, holding the ropes that would have set the boat free into the channel.

"Prepare for us to board!" the voice boomed again.

Henny's heart sank as Erik and his partner jumped onto Gerda.

The second Nazi soldier stepped up to Henny, shining his flashlight directly in her eyes. "You didn't think we'd let you get away that easily, did you? My young comrade here is far more trusting than I am." He fixed his eyes on Erik, who squirmed under his stare.

"Let's just take a look at those supplies that you're carrying," he continued. "I want to make sure there isn't any illegal cargo down below."

An icy chill ran down Henny's back. "What do you mean?"

"We've had some reports that there may be Jews trying to escape from Copenhagen. After tomorrow, there won't be any left to get away. But that's another story," he said with a chuckle. "In the meantime, we're clamping down on that sort of thing."

Just when she thought they were going to get away, everything had turned once again. The Jewish families were about to be discovered. They would be arrested and taken away. And Henny knew that she, Lukas, Otto, and Gerhardt were going to be arrested as well. And who knew what their fate would be? All she could do now was to try and delay the inevitable. She cleared her throat and shook her head. "I wouldn't know anything about Jews escaping," she said. "Like I said, we're heading to the lighthouse."

"Of course," Erik's partner replied. "Nevertheless, I'd like you to open the hold."

No one moved.

"Or would you rather I do it for you?"

At that, he raised his rifle and pointed it in Henny's direction. Then, he moved over to the hold and motioned Erik to join him. Together, they began to remove the ropes, oars, life jackets, and blankets that had been piled over the door.

Henny glanced over at Otto, still on shore, still holding the ropes. She locked eyes with him. *Make a run for it*, her eyes pleaded. If the families were discovered, at least he would be able to save himself. Otto frowned and shook his head slightly. Then, he set his mouth in a tight line and crossed his arms in front of him. He was not going anywhere.

She looked at Gerhardt. He looked as if he was ready to pounce on Erik and his partner. But what good would that do? He could never overpower the two soldiers. And Henny wasn't sure she would be able to help. And Lukas with his rifle was stuck below.

And then, she thought about Susanne—waiting in the hold, trusting her with her life. And the resolve to fight back returned, surging through her like the tide. No matter what, she could not let her friend down. If Otto and Gerhardt fought, then Henny would fight too—with her last breath, if necessary. She steeled herself as Erik removed the last blanket from on top of the door to the hold. He pulled on the padlock and turned to Henny, extending his hand.

"The key?"

Shakily, she reached into her pocket and extracted the key, dropping it into Erik's palm. "You won't find anything," she said, trying to keep her voice as light and steady as possible.

"We'll see." Erik twisted the key in the lock, removed the padlock, and flung it aside.

Henny looked down at Otto and then over at Gerhardt. All three of them stood with their fists clenched, leaning forward, ready to rush the soldiers if the families were discovered. Henny squared her shoulders and gritted her teeth, feeling the fire in her belly ignite and grow. She was ready for anything.

Erik grabbed the handle to the door and pulled it open, and in that moment, the most disgusting smell wafted up from inside the hold, like old socks mixed with rotting eggs, something dead and decaying.

It hung in the air like a bad cloud and then floated across the deck. Erik recoiled.

"What is that?" he cried, taking a step back. He fumbled to pull a handkerchief from his pocket and brought it up to his nose.

His partner took a step toward the hold and flinched. He jumped back and turned his face away. "Did something die in there?"

"It's fish," Henny said. "The people at the lighthouse requested it. That's why we need to get moving," she added. "We've got to get it refrigerated before it all goes bad."

Erik was still holding his nose. "It smells like you're too late."

His partner stepped toward the hold once more, but quickly retreated. "That's disgusting. I'm not going down there."

Henny couldn't believe it! It was a moment of salvation. But a second later, the soldier turned to Erik. "You go down and check to see what's below."

"Me?" Erik stammered.

"It's an order," the soldier bellowed as Henny's hopes evaporated once more.

Erik moved toward the hold, still pressing the handkerchief up against his face. He peered down the stairs and then cringed again. "There are too many boxes," he said weakly.

"Just push them aside and get below." The second soldier was losing his patience.

Henny remained still, waiting to see what would happen, praying this would all end soon.

Erik moved closer to the steps, bending to begin moving the boxes. But just as he was about to lift the box of decaying fish, he grimaced, grabbed his stomach, and ran for the side of the boat. "I can't do it. I'm going to be sick!"

His partner hesitated, glancing from Henny to Erik, who was still doubled over. At first, Henny was afraid that he was going to order her or Gerhardt to remove the box of fish. But then, the smell simply seemed to get the better of him as well. He gagged, lowered his rifle, and stepped back.

That was Henny's cue to rush forward and close the door to the hold. A moment later, Gerhardt retrieved the padlock, reinserted it, and locked it with a firm click.

They all stood staring at one another. Henny held her breath; she didn't know what was going to happen next. Finally, the second soldier grabbed the key from Erik and extended it back to Henny.

"All right," he said gruffly. "Nothing could live down there with that smell. Get this boat out of here."

"It's going to take me days to get that stench off my body," Erik muttered.

Before leaving the boat, he turned to Henny one more time. He still looked pale and unsteady. "Maybe I'll see you around," he said weakly.

I hope not, Henny thought. She smiled briefly at Erik and said nothing.

Finally, he and his partner clicked their heels together. Both extended their arms straight in front of them in a Nazi salute. Without waiting for a response, they turned, jumped off the boat, and side by side, they marched away from the pier.

CHAPTER 26

For a moment, no one moved. Henny closed her eyes. Her head was still pounding and her heart racing, but she felt dizzy with relief. She could not believe what had just happened, how close they had come to a disaster, and how lucky they were that the families hadn't been discovered. She breathed in and out, hoping the familiar sea air would work its magic and steady her. When she finally opened her eyes, Gerhardt was standing in front of her.

"We need to get out of here," he said, all business.

Henny shook her head one more time, trying to clear away the memory of what had just happened. Then, she called out to Otto, still on shore. He, too, looked stunned, mouth open, frozen like a statue on the dock, still holding a rope in his hands.

"What are you waiting for?" Henny cried. "Let's go!"

That did it. Otto sprang into action, threw the ropes on board, and jumped on after them. He moved to take his position at the bow, and Gerhardt at the stern. Henny walked back into the cabin and turned the key in the ignition. The motor came alive with a thunderous roar. Then, she eased the *Gerda III* away from the pier and began to maneuver her into the channel.

The rain that had started earlier that evening had stopped. Stars were beginning to emerge from behind the clearing, revealing a bright sky. Henny knew that she should probably be worried about the lack of cloud cover. The risk of being seen on the water had suddenly increased. But after having just skirted the catastrophe of being searched by Erik and his Nazi partner, she figured a clear sky was a message that there would be clear sailing ahead. She welcomed the star-filled darkness above her like an old friend.

It was only when they had passed the lighthouse and Henny could make out details of the gray rocky coastline of Sweden up ahead that she finally had

Otto unlock the hold. She relinquished the steering wheel to Gerhardt and went out on deck. She barely noticed the smell when Otto removed the box of fish along with the other boxes that were blocking the staircase. All she could think about was seeing the faces of her passengers and feeling the relief of knowing they were fine.

"We're only about a half an hour away," Henny announced when the boxes had been cleared and she had walked down the stairs to face the families.

Mr. and Mrs. Meyer looked dazed and pale. Mrs. Meyer held Raquel's hand. Their young son, Martin, was just beginning to stir. Tears were flowing down Mrs. Meyer's cheeks. "We're so relieved," she muttered.

Mr. Hertz struggled to his feet, trying to find a place for his head between the low beams. Henny reached out a hand to help him, but he brushed it aside. "I can manage quite well on my own, young lady," he said. Then he smiled at her. "But I do want to thank you as well." He grasped his wife by the arm and pulled her up to stand beside him. "My wife and I will never forget what you've done for us."

Mr. Rubin still had baby Aron nestled against his shoulder. Susanne was seated between her parents, staring up at Henny.

"Are you all right?" Henny asked, bending to face Susanne.

She nodded. "I'm glad that's over."

Henny smiled. "Me too."

"We heard it all," Mr. Rubin said. "When the door to the hold opened, I thought it was the end for us."

"You have Otto to thank for preventing those soldiers from searching any further," Henny said. "That rotting herring drove them back."

"It was an ingenious plan," added Mr. Hertz. "But it's good to have that box out of there. The smell of that fish was starting to choke me." Otto had already moved the box of fish to the stern of the boat, as far away from the hold as possible. Henny had asked him to bring something to eat down to her passengers. Now, he carried flasks of hot tea down the stairs along with cheese and bread that they had stored on board just for this moment. This time, the families devoured everything that was offered to them.

Finally, Henny turned to Lukas, who still held his rifle. His blond bangs fell across his forehead and he pushed them back with one hand. "That was close," he said.

Henny sighed deeply. "I know."

"You and I have had a couple of close calls."

She nodded. "I know that too."

Lukas made a move to sit back down when Henny stopped him. A smile tugged at the corners of her mouth. "Your job isn't over yet," she said with as much authority as she could muster. "I need you to come up on deck and be my lookout; watch the water for any sign of danger."

Lukas sprang back to his feet and grinned. "I'm on it, Captain."

"You were right," Henny added as Lukas passed her. "We do make a pretty good team."

Then, Henny turned back to Susanne. "I need some help steering this boat to Sweden. Do you think there's anyone on board who can give me a hand?"

A wide smile spread across Susanne's face. "I can help!"

"Do you think it's safe to take Susanne out of here?" Mrs. Rubin asked. She glanced anxiously at Henny. "Won't the Nazis see her if one of their boats is out there?"

Henny knew that the worst of the danger was over. They were close to Sweden and no other boats were in sight. She explained this to Mrs. Rubin, who finally nodded her agreement.

Henny took Susanne by the hand and escorted her up the stairs. Lukas was waiting for her at the top.

"Look at what you've been able to do," he said. His eyes shone with admiration.

"What *we've* been able to do," Henny corrected. "You're the one who got me into this resistance business in the first place."

"Something tells me you would have found your way in, with or without me."

"I don't know about that. You were there at the start of all of this, and you're here with me now. I'm glad you are."

He reached out and squeezed her hand. His eyes met hers and rested there.

"I hope other Jewish families are able to get away," Henny added, feeling the warmth spread across her face.

"Well, once we deposit these people safely on the other side, I think we're going to have to come back and do it all over again."

Henny startled. She hadn't thought beyond this mission. But Lukas was right. There were other Jewish families who needed to escape. And if she could, she wanted to help them. She looked up at Lukas, eyes shining as brightly as the stars above. "Yes," she replied. "As many times as we can."

Just then, she felt a tug on her arm. When she looked down, Susanne was grinning up at her.

Together, they walked into the cabin. Gerhardt happily turned the steering wheel over to Henny, and then ran to get the small box that he had placed under Susanne's feet the last time she had gone out on the water.

"Do you remember all that I taught you the last time we sailed?" Henny asked.

"Oh, yes!"

Susanne stepped up in front of Henny. "Ten o'clock and two o'clock," she said, reaching up and placing her hands on the steering wheel. "Come on, Gerda," she added. "I need your help to do this."

In response, the *Gerda III* slid through the waves. Susanne laughed out loud, and a moment later, Henny joined in. Then, she clasped her hands over Susanne's, and together they sailed the Gerda and its passengers to freedom.

WHO WAS HENNY SINDING?

Henny grew up sailing boats in the channel beside her home city of Copenhagen in Denmark. Her father, a young navy officer, inspired Henny with his own passion for the sea. The channel between Denmark and Sweden was Henny's refuge. She raced sailboats and Dragon sloops, eventually working her way up to sailing her father's boat, the *Gerda III*, a forty-foot vesel that made daily runs to bring supplies to the Drogden Lighthouse at the south end of the channel.

The Nazis invaded Denmark in 1940, but they ran the country in a relatively laid-back manner. Danish citizens were free to continue working and running their own businesses, King Christian X continued to rule, and the Jewish citizens of Denmark lived with few restrictions. All of that changed in 1943 when Hitler instituted martial law in Denmark, clamped down on resisters, and ordered the Gestapo to round up all of its Jewish citizens for deportation to the concentration camps. The date chosen for the roundup was October 1, which was Rosh Hashanah, one of the holiest days for Jewish people.

The truth is that most Danish citizens hated the Nazis and everything they stood for. They also valued and respected their Jewish citizens. When Henny heard that Jews were going to be arrested and deported to the concentration camps, she decided that she would do everything in her power to save as many Jewish families as possible. Starting in September 1943, Henny and the *Gerda III* made more than twenty crossings from Copenhagen to Sweden, then a neutral country. She is thought to have saved over 300 Jewish citizens. In real life, she was twenty-two years old when she began sailing Jews to Sweden. For the purpose of this story, I have made her younger.

Henny was not the only one to help the Jews of Demark. A nationwide effort took place to rescue Jews using more than 300 Danish boats. Of the roughly 8,000 Jews who lived in Denmark during the war, more than 7,700 were saved, though few boats rescued as many people as the *Gerda III*.

Henny's efforts in the Resistance during that time were not limited to saving Jews on board Gerda. She also conducted other missions throughout Denmark, helping to blow up factories, distribute anti-Nazi pamphlets, and raid Nazi facilities. She finally was forced to escape herself, or risk arrest.

She left Denmark for Sweden, where she eventually married and had children. She passed away in 2009 but continued to race sailboats for many years after the war ended.

The *Gerda III* sailed with the Danish Lighthouse and Buoy Service for another forty-one years after the end of the war. The Danish government then donated the boat to the Museum of Jewish Heritage in New York City, where it was restored. Today, the boat is housed in Connecticut's Mystic Seaport Museum. Boat experts continue to display the boat and talk about its remarkable history, and the brave young woman who once stood at its helm.

Kathy Kacer is the author of more than twenty-five books for young readers. A winner of the Silver Birch, Red Maple, and National Jewish Book Awards in Canada and the U.S., Kathy has written unforgettable stories inspired by real events. She lives in Toronto, Ontario.